"You're jealous."

Dear Diary:

Nancy was glaring at me and I thought she was going to yell. But then she shook her head and took another bite of her sandwich. How she can eat when we're fighting is one of life's unsolved mysteries. "You know what?" she said with her mouth full.

"What?"

"You're jealous, that's all. Because I like to have fun. You're so worried about being cool, and doing better than Samantha at the fair, and impressing Billy, that you don't have any fun. And you don't want anybody else to have any, either."

At that moment, Diary, I wished Nancy had never become my roommate.

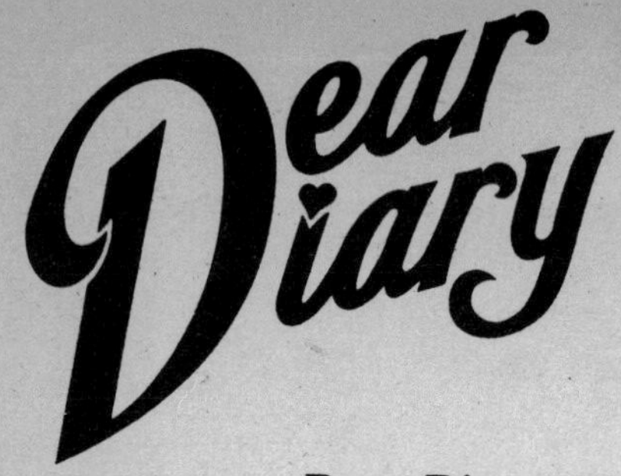

Dear Diary #1: The Party

Dear Diary #2: The Secret

Dear Diary #3: The Dance

Dear Diary #4: The Mystery

Dear Diary #5: The Roommate

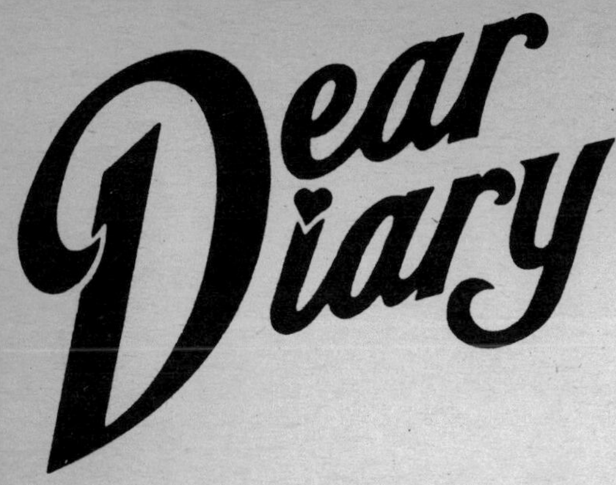

THE ROOMMATE

Carrie Randall

AN
APPLE
PAPERBACK

SCHOLASTIC INC.
New York Toronto London Auckland Sydney

ISBN 0-590-44023-3

12 11 10 9 8 7 6 5 4 3 2 1 1 2 3 4 5 6/9

Printed in the U.S.A. 40

First Scholastic printing, March 1991

KEEP OUT!!

(This means you!)

This diary is the property of

Elizabeth Jane Miletti

ALL TRESPASSERS WILL BE PROSECUTED!

1

Dear Diary:

Do you know what I'd like right now, more than anything in the world? My own phone. Not just an extension, either, but my very own private line that only I can use. I can see the listing now: "Miletti, Elizabeth." No, I'd make it "Miletti, Liz." At least the phone book would use the name *I* want. Not Lizzie, which is what the whole world calls me no matter how much I like "Liz."

Of course, my name doesn't have anything to do with why I want a phone. The real reason I want one is that I always need to talk to Nancy. And you can imagine what kind of reaction that got when I mentioned it at dinner tonight!

"You're only eleven," my father said. "I thought we had at least a couple of years before you started asking for a phone."

"Does that mean I'll get one when I'm thirteen?" I asked.

"I'm thirteen already," my brother Adam reminded me. "I'd have to get one first."

"Well, I'm sixteen, and I don't have one," my older brother Josh said.

"Neither one of you has asked," my mother commented. "And don't even bother," she told them with a grin.

Darcy peered into a serving bowl and stuck out her tongue. "Daddy, what *is* this stuff?" she asked.

Darcy's eight, as you know, Diary, and her manners aren't the greatest. This time, though, I couldn't blame her. The bowl was filled with these flat round things that looked sort of like tie-dyed floppy disks. Another new Roth Frozen Food that my father was testing on us.

"Roth is calling them Paisley Potato Patties," Dad said. "The potatoes are grated with red and green peppers, then shaped into patties." He stared at them for a second. "I don't think the paisley pattern came through too well."

"Yuk, I hate peppers," Darcy remarked.

"Darcy." Mom frowned at her, but I could tell her heart wasn't in it. Mom's more patient than anybody with the weird stuff Dad brings home from work, but I noticed she only took one Paisley Potato.

"Yum!" Rose had already scarfed down two of them and now she was reaching for more.

"That's my baby," Dad said.

"Rose is four," Josh pointed out. "When are we going to stop calling her the baby?"

"When she asks us to," Dad said, "and not a minute sooner."

Rose ate another potato and then dug into the spinach. She has to be the only four-year-old who'll eat the stuff. But she'll eat anything; that's why we call her the Human Garbage Disposal.

I ate a Paisley Potato (not bad, but I don't think it's going to be a hot seller), and cleared my throat. "About the phone," I said. "I know I can't have one of my own, but I really do have to call Nancy, so can I have first dibs on it after dinner?"

"It's your turn to load the dishwasher," Mom reminded me.

"Okay, after that," I said.

"After that, homework," she said.

I groaned. "I won't talk long, I promise."

"Never make a promise you can't keep," Josh told me. He can be *so* stuffy sometimes.

Dad laughed. "Lizzie, you go to school with Nancy. You're *in* school with her, and then you walk home together after school. Isn't that enough time to communicate?"

Before I could answer, Darcy announced that she needed to use the phone, too. "I have to tell Patty I'm coming to her birthday party."

"Darcy!" I said. "You can tell Patty tomorrow at school."

"I don't want to wait," Darcy argued. "Besides, *I* don't have any homework."

"If I have to wait, so do you," I said.

"Mom!" Darcy cried.

"Take my advice and don't whine," Josh told her. "It doesn't help."

"Mom!" Darcy said again.

"Okay, enough," Mom said. "This started out as a pleasant dinner, but it's going downhill fast. So here's the solution: Nobody makes any calls tonight except in an emergency."

Mom wasn't mad; she just wanted the subject dropped. But it didn't work. Darcy got all pouty and Josh said he absolutely *had* to make a call about some plans for a weekend party. He probably needed to find out if Mary Lou Witty, the girl he's madly in love with, was going to be there. Even Rose decided she wanted to call Gram!

Adam was the only one of us kids who didn't join in. While everybody else was complaining, he quietly fed his Paisley Potatoes to our dog, Sebastian, who was lurking under the table. The cats, Marilyn Monroe and Elvis, were there, too, but they each took one sniff and stalked away.

So that's how it went, Diary. I loaded the dishwasher, and then came up here to my room and did my homework. Most of it was easy, except for history, which is my worst subject. Mr. Burrows told us to be on the lookout for a pop quiz sometime this week, so I knew I couldn't put off reading the chapter on Westward Expansion. If I flunk another quiz, I'll be in big trouble in that class. Again.

After I finally slogged my way through the chapter, and across the Mississippi, I practiced the piano, keeping one ear out for the phone. I was sure Nancy would call me, and Mom's rule was only about *making* calls, not taking them. But if Nancy tried, she wouldn't have been able to get through. All the salespeople in the country must have picked this night to try to sell us magazine subscriptions and storm windows and vacation condominiums.

Now it's ten-thirty and too late for telephone calls anyway, even if we could make them. I know I shouldn't feel grumpy about this, but you see the problem? It's not that my call to Nancy was an emergency. But with five kids and two adults, you kind of get lost in the crowd sometimes. You need somebody who pays attention just to you.

When Gram lived upstairs in the attic apartment, before she married Ralph Bagnold and moved to his house, she used to do that. If she was still here, I'd be up there now, talking to her, and probably eating some of her great brownies.

But I'd still want to talk to my best friend. I guess that's why Nancy Underpeace and I *are* best friends — because we're always ready to listen. Well, almost always. I mean, we *do* have fights. We're so different. I wish I could be more sophisticated, more grown up, I guess. And Nancy'd be happy to stay eleven forever. She says she's good at being a kid and doesn't want to change. So she doesn't understand sometimes when I talk about wanting to be cool, and how exciting it'll be when we get into junior high, or even just when I make a big deal about what to wear. And I get annoyed because she still likes to ride her bike to school, even though almost nobody else in sixth grade does anymore, and she couldn't care less about clothes or boys.

So sometimes the differences lead to fights. But we always make up. And I need to talk to her, because I'm really excited about something, and I'm pretty sure Nancy will be, too.

It happened after school today. Dad was wrong — Nancy and I don't *always* walk home together. Today she had to go to her reading tutor, because she's dyslexic. As I was walking down the hall, Samantha "The Snob" Howard and her two friends, Candace Quinn and Jessica Aldridge, were right behind me.

"Is that Lizzie Miletti?" I heard Candace say.

"I think it is!" Jessica said. "I almost don't recognize her when she's without Nancy."

I turned around and smiled. I don't really like them, but I've decided part of being cool is acting like you're not insulted. "Hi, you guys."

Samantha shook her long, curly blonde hair back. "We're going shopping at the mall, Lizzie. You wouldn't be headed that way, too, would you?"

I knew Samantha wasn't inviting me, since she can't stand me. I'm pretty sure she's *never* liked me, but it's gotten worse since the sixth-grade dance, when I was asked to dance and she wasn't. But even if she had been inviting me, I wouldn't have accepted.

"No," I said. "There's always too much homework on Mondays."

Candace giggled. "That doesn't stop us!"

Nothing stops them, I thought. They all have plenty of money, especially Samantha. "Well, have fun," I said, as we went out the doors.

"Bye-bye!" Samantha waved her fingers at me and the three of them walked off together.

I sighed. Nancy thinks those three are jerks, and most of the time, I agree with her. But watching Samantha, I couldn't help wishing I looked a little more like her, or a least had the kind of fashion sense she does. Snob or not, she dresses great. Today, she had on a short yellow skirt, and a yellow-and-black striped sweater. At lunch, Nancy said she looked like a giant bumblebee, but I thought she looked very dramatic.

I was looking down at *my* skirt — denim, and

not short enough — when a voice behind me said, "Hi, Lizzie."

I turned around and it was Billy Watts. You know Billy, of course. He's only one of the cutest boys in sixth grade.

"Hi, Billy."

"I was looking for you," he said, still smiling. "You know the fair?"

"Sure," I said. Every year, Claremont Elementary School has a fair to help raise money for something. Last year it was for new swings for the playground. This year it's for more library books.

"Well, my mom's on the committee," he said. "And she's going crazy trying to get people to come up with ideas for booths and then work in them. You know — a ring toss, clown makeup for the little kids, stuff like that."

I nodded.

"I told her I'd ask some of the kids in class," he said. "A couple of them said okay, but most of them don't want to. But anyway, I thought maybe you might be interested."

Now since I'm always totally honest with you, Diary, I have to tell you, I really wasn't interested. I mean, I stopped going to the school fair after fourth grade. It's really for the little kids.

But then I told myself that *working* in a booth

at the fair was very different from just *going* to the fair. It meant you were a responsible person, which is part of growing up, or so my parents are always telling us.

Also, Billy was looking kind of desperate, and I felt like I couldn't turn him down. And since I'm being honest, I have to tell you that part of the reason I said yes was because I have a crush on Billy (me and just about every other girl in sixth grade). I knew he'd already asked other kids, but it made me feel special to have him ask me.

So I said yes. And Billy grinned, sort of punched me on the arm, and told me he knew I'd come up with a really great idea for a booth.

Which is my problem. I haven't been able to think of a single good idea. I'm not stupid, but I'm not the most creative person in the world. Ideas have to sort of hit me over the head. When I *try* to think of them, my mind goes blank.

But Nancy is full of ideas. Every time there's a special project, like for science or history, the teachers always *ooh* and *ahh* over hers. Plus, she loves the school fair. She doesn't care if nobody else thinks it's cool anymore, she goes and tosses beanbags and throws darts with all the little kids and has a great time.

So that's why I want to talk to her so much. Not only will she come up with a terrific idea for a booth, but she'll understand how I feel — about Billy. When something happens that is important, you just want to tell your best friend. Who else can you share your feelings with?

You, Diary. Thank goodness!

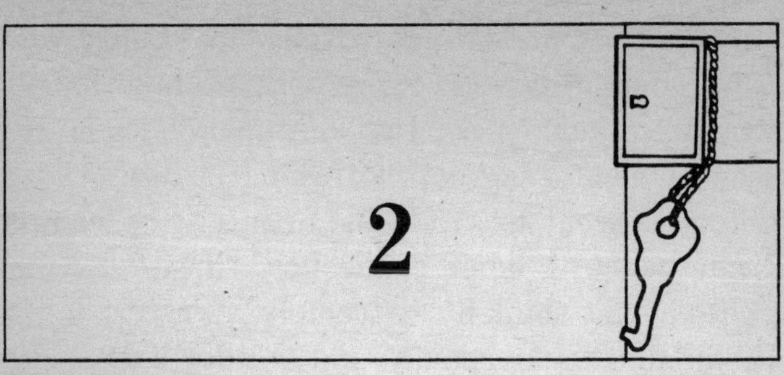

2

Dear Diary:

What a great day! No pop quiz in history (yet), pizza for lunch (the cafeteria actually does a decent job on it), and a B+ from Mr. Rice on my book report in English. And those are just the little things!

I'll start from the beginning.

Nancy was waiting for me at the corner this morning, as usual. It was chilly out, and she was wearing this stretched-out gray sweatshirt jacket that probably belonged to her father once upon a time. Like I said, Nancy doesn't think much about clothes.

She didn't have the hood up and her long, straight blonde hair was blowing in the wind. As I walked toward her, I wished for about the millionth time that I had her hair, instead of my dark frizzy mop. I also wouldn't mind borrowing a few inches from her. I'm short (considerate people would say petite), and Nancy's the tallest girl in class. Willowy, to be polite.

Both of us are always wishing we could trade looks, but I have to confess, there's one thing I wouldn't trade — no, two. I wouldn't trade my eyes, which are green with long lashes. And I definitely wouldn't trade last names. Nancy hates Underpeace. I don't blame her, since very *im*polite people think it's extremely witty to call her things like "Underpants" and "Undertaker."

Anyway, when I reached her, she said, "Is your phone out of order or something? I tried to call you about fifteen times last night and the line was always busy."

"I knew it!" I said. We started walking together and I explained about Mom's one-night rule, and all the sales pitches we got. "Why did you call?" I asked.

"Nothing special," she said. "I just felt like talking. Mom couldn't understand it — she said we're together all day, why couldn't we get our talking done then?"

"That's exactly what Dad said," I told her. "Maybe there's some kind of handbook they all read. You know — 'Frustrating Responses to Your Child's Reasonable Requests.' "

"Probably," Nancy mumbled. She wasn't really paying attention. She was looking at the highest branches of an extremely tall tree. She'd spotted a bird, for sure. Nancy's crazy about bird-watching. I've gone with her to the nature preserve a few times, and it's actually very peaceful. For excitement, though, I still think it ranks somewhere between watching the grass grow and waiting for water to boil.

"Too bad I don't have my binoculars with me," Nancy sighed, after mentioning some kind of speckled species.

"Forget the birds for a minute," I told her. "We've got to start thinking about the school fair."

" 'We'?" She gave me a funny look. "I've been thinking about it, but I thought you'd decided it was too babyish. Don't tell me you're going to go with me this year."

"Well . . ." I cleared my throat. "Not exactly."

Nancy turned around and started walking backwards, grinning at me. "Okay, Lizzie Miletti. What is it? You look worried and excited at the same time. What's it got to do with the school fair?"

I took a deep breath and told her everything. I even admitted how special it made me feel to have Billy ask me. Then I crossed my fingers and waited for her reaction.

"Puppets," was the first thing she said.

I was so worried she'd accuse me of being boy-crazy — which I'm *not* — that I honestly thought she was calling me a puppet, and letting Billy Watts pull the strings. "Nancy Underpeace, you know that's not true!" I said loudly. "Just because

I happen to think about boys once in a while doesn't mean I'm — "

"What are you talking about, Lizzie?" Nancy stopped walking backwards and stared at me. "You say you need a great idea for a fair booth and I say 'puppets' and you start babbling about boys!"

It took a second, but it finally sank into my brain. "You mean 'puppets' as in 'puppet show'?" I asked.

"Right, kind of like Punch and Judy," Nancy agreed. "We could call it 'The Halls of Claremont,' or something like that, and sort of do a spoof of some of the teachers and kids and the principal!"

"That's great!" I told her. "We can write the script together and there's a box of old clothes Mom's been meaning to take to the Goodwill — we could use some of them to make the puppets with!"

"Right, and the show will be a real farce," Nancy said. "You know, a kid running around the room, and a spitball fight, and a teacher getting hysterical because nobody did their homework. The little kids will love it!"

I was getting more and more excited about it. "We'll write lots of different scenes," I said, "instead of doing the same show over and over. That way, kids will keep coming back and the booth will make more money."

"And Billy Watts will fall on his knees in front of the entire sixth grade and kiss your hand," Nancy added.

"Very funny," I said. "I do not want him to kiss my hand."

"No, but you want him to like you."

"He already likes me," I pointed out. Then I quickly added, "He likes both of us. We're friends."

"Then why did you agree to do this?" she asked.

I was starting to get flustered, and I could feel a hideous blush creeping across my face. "Okay," I admitted. "I said yes because he asked me."

"I know — you said it made you feel special," Nancy said. "I understand. I'm just not ready to think about boys. It complicates everything. But I don't care if you are. Besides," she added, "this puppet show is going to be so much fun. I'm really glad you asked me to do it with you."

Wasn't that great, Diary? Nancy didn't call me gross or disgusting just because I happen to have a crush on Billy. Now that I think of it, having a crush is kind of fun. You don't have to worry about dating or falling in love, which is extremely scary; you just *like* somebody a little bit differently than you like anybody else.

Plus, Nancy came up with a great idea, like I knew she would. By the time we got to school, I'd almost forgotten that it was Billy who'd asked me to do a booth. We told him about it during English, and he was really glad that both of us were working on it. That made me feel good, but by then, the idea of the puppet show was so much fun that it didn't matter how the whole thing got started.

Then, at lunch, something else great happened. (Not the pizza, even though it was a nice surprise.) Samantha and Candace overheard Nancy and me talking about the puppet show. Usually they don't sit anywhere near us, but one of the fourth-grade classes got back from a field trip late, so the cafeteria was really crowded.

Samantha acted like we were invisible, but Candace kept glancing at us. Finally she asked, "What on earth are you two talking about? I keep hearing things about the first-grade teachers getting locked in their rooms, and somebody painting the office. Is this for real?"

I was tempted to say yes, but Nancy answered before I could. "No, Lizzie and I are working on ideas for a script," she said. "We're doing a puppet show for the school fair."

"Oh, the fair." Candace tucked her short black hair behind her ears and sniffed. Samantha looked bored.

"Right," Nancy said. "Billy Watts asked Lizzie personally if she would do one of the booths."

Samantha glanced at me sideways out of her

blue eyes, and then quickly stood up. Her face was kind of pink, and I knew it wasn't from the makeup she wears. She was actually blushing! She and Candace left to return their trays, and when I looked at Nancy, she had her hand over her mouth, trying not to laugh.

"I can't believe you said that," I told her.

"Well, it's true, he did ask you personally," she said with a giggle.

"But not the way you meant," I said, giggling, too. "And I thought you actually felt sorry for Samantha once in a while."

"I do," Nancy said. "I mean, I'll bet Billy didn't ask her to do a booth for the same reason none of the boys asked her to dance — because she's so perfect-looking and acts so junior high, they're scared of her. I'll bet she's lonely a lot of times."

I knew Nancy was probably right. But after the way Samantha had once tried to break up our friendship by pretending to like Nancy so much, it was hard for me to work up much sympathy for her.

"I said that about Billy because I knew it would make her jealous," Nancy admitted. "Does that make me mean?"

My mouth was full of pizza, so I shook my head. When I swallowed, I said, "I don't think so. I think it makes you human."

"I guess you're right." Then Nancy giggled

again. "Maybe there's some way we can work the Snob Queen into the script."

And now, for the best thing.

Nancy and I had just left school and we were trying to decide whether or not to stop for some ice cream, when a car screeched to a halt right behind us. It was Nancy's mother.

"Thank goodness!" Mrs. Underpeace called out the window. "I was afraid I'd miss you."

"Mom, what are you doing here?" Nancy asked.

I was surprised, too. Ever since Nancy's parents got divorced, Mrs. Underpeace has been working extra hours at her computer programming job at least two or three days a week. Nancy told me that her father pays child support, but I guess it's not always enough.

"What are you doing here?" Nancy asked again.

"Get in and I'll tell you," her mother said. "You, too, Lizzie. I'll drop you home."

After we got in, Mrs. Underpeace told us her news: The company she works for was sending her to Houston for two weeks to set up a computer program for a huge hospital. "It's a real show of faith in me," she said excitedly. "They're giving me total control over any changes that have to be made; I'll be dealing with the entire hospital staff almost. It's going to be a real challenge."

"That's great, Mom," Nancy said.

"Really," I agreed. "When are you leaving?"

"Tomorrow," Mrs. Underpeace said. "That's why I wanted to pick you up, Nancy. After we drop Lizzie off, we've got some shopping to do. I want to get a couple of lightweight outfits for the weather down there, and you've been needing some new jeans and a new pair of shoes. Then I've got to get home and pack. My plane leaves at nine in the morning."

Nancy and I were in the backseat, and we glanced at each other. I could tell what she was thinking — she'd probably go stay with her father.

She didn't look too excited, and I didn't blame her. Not that I don't like her father, and I know she loves him. It's just that he moved to Detroit after the divorce. Detroit's not very far from Hampton Point, but it's not exactly within walking distance of Claremont Elementary. Was she going to have to be away for two whole weeks?

Nancy sighed and then leaned forward toward the front seat. "So what time does my bus leave?" she asked.

"Bus?" Mrs. Underpeace glanced in the rearview mirror. "What bus?"

"The one to Detroit," Nancy said. "And does the school know I won't be here for a while?"

"You wish," her mother laughed. "No, Nancy, I'm afraid you're not getting out of school for two weeks."

"You mean I have to go to a whole new school in Detroit, just for two weeks?!"

"That would be ridiculous," Mrs. Underpeace said.

That was exactly what *I* was thinking, Diary.

Then Nancy's mother laughed again. "I've found a place right here in Hampton Point for you to stay," she said. "You can even take your cat with you. The food's good, there'll be plenty of company, and you'll be able to walk to our house every couple of days to get the mail."

Nancy was frowning, but I finally got it.

"A big frame house, right?" I asked. "One dog, two cats, five kids?"

"That's the one," Mrs. Underpeace said.

"You mean I'm staying with Lizzie?" Nancy wasn't frowning anymore. "Really?"

"Really," her mother said. "I talked to your mother this morning, Lizzie, and she said it'll be just fine. In fact, it was Lynn who suggested it." She looked in the mirror again. "I see both of you are grinning from ear to ear. I take it that means the arrangement is okay."

"Okay?" Nancy was practically bouncing around in the seat. "It's fantastic!"

Isn't it, Diary? I mean, Nancy and I *do* spend a lot of time together, but this is going to be different. We won't have to wish we could use the phone late at night, or wait until morning to tell each other something. We'll be able to talk as much as we want, whenever we want. For two whole weeks, my best friend will be my roommate!

3

Dear Diary:

If this entry is hard to read, it's because I'm writing with the tiniest amount of light I can see by and not go blind! It turns out that Nancy likes to sleep in the pitch-dark. When we were getting ready to go to sleep, I turned on my bedside lamp and after about fifteen minutes, Nancy asked me to turn it off.

"Okay," I said. "Except I always thought you could sleep no matter what. I didn't think even floodlights would wake you up."

"I guess I have to be really tired," she said. "Or maybe lights don't bother me when we're just sleeping over at each other's houses for a night. But in regular life, I like it dark."

"Regular life?"

"Yeah," she said with a big yawn. "You know, not weekends. Monday to Friday, when we have to get up for school. Regular life."

"This isn't regular," I said. "We're roommates now. It's special."

Another big yawn. "I know, but I still can't sleep with that light on."

After a few minutes of lying in the dark, I got up and went down to Josh and Adam's room. Adam was already asleep but Josh was sitting at his desk, staring at a book. I bet he wasn't really studying. I bet he was dreaming of Mary Lou Witty.

Anyway, Josh let me borrow an old clip-on bed lamp that he doesn't use anymore, and I brought it back to my room. It's about as strong as a pen-light, so it can't possibly bother Nancy. It's eleven-thirty now, and I'm yawning like crazy, but I wanted to tell you about the day, or as much as I can before I conk out.

This morning at seven-thirty, Mrs. Underpeace dropped Nancy and all her stuff (including her bike and her kitten, Oscar) at our house. Then she drove to the airport, and Nancy and I spent most of the time until school keeping Marilyn and Elvis from attacking poor Oscar.

"Maybe I should have boarded him at the vet's," Nancy said worriedly, trying to pick up her hissing cat.

I puffed a tuft of cat hair away from my mouth. By this time, hundreds of little tufts were drifting around the kitchen.

"Yuck!" Darcy shouted. "There's whole bunches of cat hair in my Cheerios! Mom!"

"Have a waffle, Darcy," Mom said, pouring juice for Rose. "Dad brought home a new kind last night. Adam, get them out of the freezer, would you?"

Adam had just taken the bag out when Marilyn and Elvis streaked past and collided with his legs. He spun around and the bag of waffles flew up into the air. Nancy was still holding a squirming Oscar under one arm, but she shot out her other hand and grabbed the bag just as it was about to crash-land on the coffeemaker.

"Nice catch!" Adam said.

"Thanks," Nancy grinned. The two of them tossed the bag back and forth a couple of times. Darcy got mad, so Nancy handed her the waffles.

"Mom!" Darcy said. "These waffles are weird-looking. What's in them?"

"Don't ask," Mom sighed.

"It's eggplant," Adam announced.

"Oh, gross!"

"Thanks, Adam," Mom said.

Just then the back door opened and Josh came in with Sebastian. The three cats took one look at the dog and suddenly they were allies. They chased Sebastian around the kitchen at least ten times before Mom finally let him take refuge in the basement. After that, the cats exchanged sniffs and went to sleep.

"Welcome to the Miletti house, Nancy." Mom laughed.

"The Miletti Fun House, she means," Adam said, punching Nancy's arm as he went out the door.

It's funny, Diary, because Nancy's stayed overnight at our house plenty of times — she knows it can get wild. But I was starting to worry. Actually living in the Miletti Fun House might be too much for her to take.

But when we finally left for school, she said, "This is going to be a great two weeks, I can tell already."

I think so, too, but I have to stop for a minute.

Would you believe it? I'm now writing in the bathroom. Nancy started turning over a lot and I didn't want her to wake up and ask me what I'm doing. I've never told her — or anyone — that I keep a diary. Even though Nancy is my very best friend, there are things I don't tell her. Not any deep, dark secrets; not yet, anyway! Just thoughts and feelings that I don't want to tell anybody, even Nancy. Except you, of course.

Anyway, back to today.

Maybe Nancy coming to stay with us is good luck — still no pop quiz in history!

"I'll bet Mr. Burrows is saving it for Friday,"

I said as we left the class with Ericka Powell. "It's just a sneaky way to make sure we read the assignment every night."

"Teachers are full of tricks like that," Ericka agreed. She didn't sound all that upset about it, but then, Ericka's very calm. Her emotions don't go up and down like mine.

"But at least now we'll be able to study together, so it won't be so bad," Nancy said to me.

"What's new about you two studying together?" Ericka asked. "You do it all the time."

"I know, but now we don't have to plan it," I said. Then I told her about Nancy staying with us.

"Neat," Ericka said. "Sort of like roommates."

"Oh, neat!" somebody behind us echoed.

It was Candace. With Samantha and Jessica, naturally. I guess they'd been listening to our conversation, hoping to hear something they could make fun of.

"Don't you two see enough of each other already?" Jessica asked. "If you actually live together, you'll be like clones."

"The Bobbsey twins," Candace giggled.

"If we're the Bobbsey twins," Nancy whispered to Ericka and me, "they're the Three Stooges."

We laughed, but I noticed that Samantha hadn't said anything. She just walked along, looking gorgeous in a hot-pink designer sweatshirt that cost forty-five dollars at Milliken's. I know because I saw it and decided the only way I'd ever be able to afford it was to rob a bank.

Anyway, Samantha kept quiet. She's been doing that a lot lately, it seems to me. Letting Candace and Jessica make the cutesy remarks and sort of acting like she's above it all.

But today, it looked like she had something else on her mind. She didn't even smile in that super-cool way she has. I hope she's not trying to think up some new scheme to make life miserable for Nancy and me. But even if she is, it wouldn't work. Especially not now that we're roommates, because we'll be able to talk all the time and there won't be any way she can come between us.

I'm back in my room. Mom saw the bathroom light and asked if I was sick. Too sleepy to write more, anyway.

Six-thirty (!) in the morning, Diary. Nancy's alarm went off with the birds (naturally) and she told me to go back to sleep while she showered, but I don't think I can. I didn't know she got up so early. She never did the other times she slept over. Of course, that was usually on weekends. I guess we'll have to get used to each other's regular-life habits.

I've never noticed because I'm usually still sound asleep, but my room looks good in the early-morning light. The sun creeps across my patchwork quilt, and the blue walls kind of glow.

Of course, it's a little crowded now. It's small anyway, and the foam chair Nancy brought that folds out into a bed leaves about two square feet of floor space. Plus, there's an extra set of clothes, books, and shoes. Nancy got a new pair of sneakers, but she brought her old checkered ones, too. She said she rescued them from the garbage just in time. I've promised myself not to tell her that they are totally out of style. If they were ever in style in the first place!

But Nancy's very neat. I mean, her room at home always looks much neater than mine, but I just figured her mom made her keep it that way. But last night after dinner she helped me clear out a space in my closet and two drawers in my dresser and lug the stuff (some of it was so ancient I wouldn't wear it anymore anyway) up to Gram's old apartment. Then she put her things away. Hanging straight and neatly folded.

This probably sounds awful, but I thought Nancy would be messy, because she doesn't care about clothes. Instead, I'm always worrying about how I look and what I've got on, but I'm the slob! It's funny what you find out about people when you live with them.

4

Dear Diary:

I've got about fifteen minutes to write. It's not midnight, either, it's only seven-thirty. I've got lots to tell, but here's why I'm not ruining my eyes trying to write in near darkness.

Earlier at dinner, Nancy and I were complaining about history. Well, *I* was complaining, but Nancy was being sympathetic. She had to be. I mean, nobody likes a pop quiz, except maybe Polly Hart, who always thinks she knows everything. And maybe Robert Wilkins, who practically *does* know everything.

"I was right," I griped. "This is Thursday, and still no quiz. He *is* going to give it to us tomorrow."

"I don't see the problem," Josh said.

"You would if you were rotten in history," I told him.

"You wouldn't be rotten if you studied harder."

Josh was right, but I made a face at him anyway.

"Lizzie, I know how you hate history," Mom

said, "but I hope you've been studying."

Nancy said, "We studied it together last night and we'll do it again tonight." She bit into what looked like a perfectly normal French fry and her eyes got real wide. "What was that?" she sputtered, reaching for her water.

"Roth's Jalapeño Fry," Dad said. "A little strip of the pepper's hidden in the middle. Too hot for you?"

Nancy was still gulping her water, but she managed to nod. "Just a little," she finally gasped.

Rose was the only one who didn't use a lot of water to wash down the fries. Her tastebuds must be coated with lead.

Anyway, after Nancy had recovered from the Jalapeño Fry, she said, "It's great studying history with Lizzie. I mean, I don't hate it like she does. I love it, but there's an awful lot of reading and that makes it hard for me sometimes. But it's not so bad when we work on it together."

"Reading!" Darcy said suddenly. "I almost forgot."

She left the table and got her backpack and pulled out a crumpled notice from the school. "Somebody has to read with me fifteen minutes every night," she announced. "It says here."

"Let me see that." Mom took the notice. "Oh, that's a good idea. 'Partners in Reading. All students in grades one through three are encouraged to read with someone — parent, friend, sitter, etc. — for fifteen minutes, a minimum of five nights a week for the next six weeks. Students who complete the program will receive recognition in the form of a Partners in Reading ribbon and a diploma.' "

"This is something new, isn't it?" Dad asked.

"It sure is," Nancy said. "If they did that when I was in first or second grade, I would have gotten caught a lot sooner."

Nancy's still embarrassed about her dyslexia, especially around other kids. I guess when almost everyone else is racing through books, it's kind of hard to explain that you see some letters backwards, or jumbled up. Plus it makes handwriting hard for her, too. But she never had any trouble talking about it in front of us. Maybe it's because nobody made a big deal about it.

"So?" Darcy asked. "Who's going to read with me?"

"Well, Darcy, the flyer says you can do the reading to somebody else," Mom told her. "How about if you read to Rose? She'd love it."

"Yeah, but she can't read back to me," Darcy said. "And I like being read to."

"I'll be glad to read to you, Darcy, but not tonight, I'm afraid," Dad said. "I've got to do a raft of paperwork for my next sales trip."

"Mom?" Darcy asked.

"Oh, honey, I can't tonight, either," Mom said. "Gram's showing some houses in that ritzy new development that I've been dying to see. So we made plans to go this evening."

Josh had swim practice. Adam had a book report to do. Darcy looked so disappointed, I was starting to feel sorry for her. I know what it's like when nobody has time for you.

Just as I was thinking that, Nancy said, "Why don't I do it? I'm supposed to read every chance I get, and besides, you said I should act like part of the family for two weeks. If everybody else is busy, I'll do it."

I was a little surprised. After dinner, Nancy and I had already decided we'd study the disgusting history, and then work on our script for the puppet show. I started to ask her if she'd forgotten, but then I decided not to. She was probably just being nice, and besides, it was only fifteen minutes.

Make that twenty-five minutes. I just came back from the kitchen, and Nancy was reading *Amelia Bedelia* to both Darcy and Rose. I think it was for the second time.

Now it's forty-five minutes. Another trip to the kitchen. No Nancy.

I went back to my room and started studying the stupid history by myself. But then I started to get a little worried. I was just about to go outside when Nancy came into the room. Her hair was all tangled and she looked hot and sweaty.

"There you are," I said. "What happened?"

"What do you mean?"

"I couldn't find you," I said, sitting up on the bed. "You finished reading and disappeared."

Nancy pushed her hair out of her eyes and looked at the clock. "Gosh, I didn't think I was out there that long."

"Out where?"

"The driveway," she laughed. "I didn't disappear. Adam finished his book report and we went out and shot some baskets."

I laughed, too. "Okay, where were you really?"

"I told you," she said. "And if you don't believe me, ask Adam. I almost beat him. Boy, was he surprised."

So was I, Diary. I guess I shouldn't have been, though. I mean, Nancy likes doing stuff like that.

"Well, anyway," I said, "it's getting kind of late. Do you want to skip the history and do the fun stuff first?"

"I'd love to," Nancy said, flopping down on her chair bed. "But I guess we better not."

That didn't surprise me. Nancy's much more

disciplined than I am, and I knew she was right. So we spent an hour on history, and then we started on the puppet show.

It's going to be great! We're calling it "The Klaremont Krazies," and so far, we've got three scenes pretty much worked out. One of them takes place in the main hall. Another one's in the office, and the third one's in the cafeteria.

At first we had about six puppets in each scene, but then we realized we only have four hands between us, so we had to cut out a bunch of characters. We've only got two voices, too, but Nancy is really great at that.

We want to have a scene in the gym and a classroom and maybe a bathroom, if we can get away with it. If we can't, then a locker room.

More to come.

Nancy's asleep now, but when I turned on the little lamp a while ago, she woke up. It was almost like a bell had gone off.

"What is it? What happened?" she asked in a very clear voice.

I jumped and stuffed you under my pillow. "I thought you were asleep," I whispered.

"I was, but I heard this really loud snap or crack," she said. "Is it windy? Maybe a branch broke outside or something."

Diary, the only snap was when I turned on the

lamp, and that was about as loud as a ballpoint pen clicking open! I never knew she had super-sensitive ears.

"It was just me," I explained. "I turned on this teeny-tiny light. I did it last night and you didn't wake up."

"Well, I woke up tonight. Anyway, why do you have it on?" she asked. "Don't tell me you're going to read more history?"

"No." That wouldn't be such a bad idea, but I couldn't possibly. "Sometimes I kind of like a little light when I sleep," I said.

"Oh." Nancy yawned loudly. "I never knew that."

"Can you sleep with it on?" I asked.

"I can try." She yawned again and pulled her pillow over her head. That made me feel guilty, so I got a towel out of the hall closet and draped it over the lamp. But then I couldn't see well enough to write, so I decided to come up here, to Gram's apartment.

I hope nobody heard me. They'll probably think there's a burglar. Or a ghost. Actually, there is a ghost. Gram's ghost.

Even though Claudine Ferrand lived here for a while when she was working at Roth's, I still think of it as Gram's apartment. If I shut my eyes, I can almost see her. I still really miss having her right upstairs from my room, but I know she's happy with Ralph. I was so afraid when she married him and moved out that I would lose her somehow. But I was wrong. We might not see each other quite as much, but we're as close as ever. I know if I need her, she'll always have time for me.

I wish Nancy and I had had more time tonight. I really hoped we could get a lot more done on the puppet show. It's next Saturday and it's not going to be easy to get everything ready. If Nancy hadn't volunteered to read and then played basketball, we might have written another scene at least.

But I also thought we'd spend some time just gabbing, the way we always do when she sleeps over. But after we got in bed, the conversation went like this:

Me: Did you notice how quiet Samantha's been the last couple of days?

Nancy: I try to notice as little as possible about that person.

Me: Well, take my word for it, she's been quiet. Every time I look at her, I can practically hear the wheels turning. She's got something on her mind.

Nancy: You mean she has one?

Me: And today I saw her talking with Billy. Smiling and tilting her head so her hair all fell to one side. (The worst part, Diary, was that Billy was smiling back. But I didn't mention that.) I bet she's planning a big party or something and she was inviting him.

Nancy: Mm.

Me: I wonder if all the boys she invites will go. *I'd* go, if I were invited, which I won't be, of course. It's because Samantha's cool, and you think maybe some of that coolness will rub off on you. You don't like her, but you kind of wish you could *be* more like her.

I didn't say anything more to Nancy because by the time I'd finished talking about Samantha's party (if it even exists), Nancy was asleep.

I guess she was tired from shooting baskets with Adam.

5

Dear Diary:

Friday at last. Nancy and I just finished peeling potatoes and making a salad for dinner. She is biking over to her house now to take in the mail and water the plants and stuff. So I've got a little time to write, without hiding out in Gram's apartment or the bathroom!

You would not believe what happened in history today!

There we were, with eighteen minutes before the class was over. And no quiz! Mr. Burrows was trying to get a discussion going about Lewis and Clark, but Robert Wilkins was the only one who was joining in. Everybody else was watching the clock and silently hoping that Robert would keep spouting until the bell rang.

I *thought* everybody else was doing that, anyway. It's only normal, right? Wrong. With fifteen minutes to go, Robert stopped two seconds to take a breath.

Two seconds was all Polly Hart needed to ruin

everything. “Mr. Burrows?” she said, waving her hand in the air like a flag.

“Yes, Polly?”

“This is Friday,” she announced, as if nobody knew how to read a calendar. “Are we going to have a pop quiz or not?”

“Will somebody gag her?” Nancy said from behind me.

“It’s too late,” Donald Harrington said.

“I just wanted to know!” Polly said as the rest of us booed and glared and muttered threats at her. “Mr. Burrows said to be ready for a quiz this week! I just wanted to know if we’re going to have it!”

“All right, everybody.” Mr. Burrows was chuckling. “Take out a sheet of paper and answer the following questions. And take that murderous look out of your eyes, too,” he added. “If you have a quiz this week — and do reasonably well — chances are you won’t have one next week. You can be grateful that Polly saved you from that.”

Grateful? I was still fuming about it at lunch. “I honestly don’t think she gets why everybody was mad,” I griped, looking over at Polly, who was sitting with Tanya Malone and talking her ear off. Tanya’s kind of a nerd — I mean, she brings cold beets for lunch and then actually eats them — but I felt sorry for her at that moment, having to listen to the traitor. “Doesn’t she know there’s an unwritten rule that you never remind a teacher of anything, unless it's something good, like an early-dismissal day?"

"Forget it, Lizzie," Ericka said. "It's over."

"That's easy for you to say," I told her. "You probably did great on the quiz. If I don't get a C or better, it really is over for me."

"What is this, anyway?" Nancy was staring at her lunch tray. We'd both bought lunch because there wasn't a single crust of bread left in the Miletti house this morning, so we couldn't make sandwiches. "It looks like meat loaf but it smells like dog food."

"It's probably both," Ericka said.

"Anyway," I went on, "I'm going to have to spend the entire weekend worrying about whether I passed."

"No, you're not," Ericka told me. "Just put it out of your mind."

"She's right," Nancy agreed. "We studied plenty, and I bet you passed."

"Okay," I said. "I'll put Polly Hart and her incredibly big mouth out of my mind. At least, I'll try. How should I do it?"

"Close your eyes and concentrate on something nice," Ericka said. "Something peaceful and pleasant."

I shut my eyes and waited for a peaceful image

to enter my mind. But before even five seconds had passed, there was a burst of laughter somewhere nearby and I had to look.

It was not something peaceful and pleasant, Diary. It was Samantha, Candace, and Jessica. They were talking to Billy. Or rather, Samantha was talking to Billy, and her two ladies-in-waiting were hanging on every word, as if she were the most fascinating person in the world. Billy, I noticed, didn't look bored either.

"I thought she invited him yesterday," I muttered.

"Invited him where?" Ericka asked.

"To her party."

Nancy reached into my bag of corn chips. She'd given up on the meat loaf, if that's what it was. "I didn't know The Queen was having a party," she said.

"Well, I'm not actually sure she is," I said. "But the reason you don't know what I'm talking about is because you played basketball with Adam," I told her.

"Huh?"

"Well, you fell asleep while I was telling you about it last night," I said. "I thought you must be really tired."

Nancy shook her head. "I wasn't that tired," she said. "I'm just used to going to sleep earlier than you on school nights because I usually shower in the morning. Did I really fall asleep while you were talking?"

"Yeah, but then you woke up immediately, the second I turned on that teeny little light," I reminded her.

"I did? I don't remember that at all."

Ericka laughed. "I thought for sure you guys would be up really late talking every night."

I did, too, Diary. But I'm discovering that having a roommate is very different from having Nancy just sleep over. You find out little things about a person that you never knew before.

But anyway, I know we'll have time over the weekend for some really marathon talks.

Plus, we've got to work on the puppet show, which has become more important than ever. Why? Because of Samantha Howard, who else?

On the way home from school, Nancy and I decided to stop in MacDermott's stationery store to get some big rolls of white paper and some paint so we could make the backdrops for the puppet show booth.

When we got inside, Mr. MacDermott, who's old and very nice (I bought my first diary from him, remember? And Gram gave me you), wasn't behind the counter. So Nancy and I started looking for the paints, and when we found them we found Mr. MacDermott.

He was standing right in front of the kind of paint we needed, and next to him was Samantha.

"She's probably going to paint a self-portrait," Nancy whispered.

I couldn't help giggling, and Mr. MacDermott looked up. Samantha did, too, and her blue eyes got all shiny. I was never sure what a glint looked like before, but now I am. There was a definite glint in Samantha's eyes.

"I'll be with you girls in a moment," Mr. MacDermott said.

"Oh, that's all right, Mr. M.," Samantha said sweetly. "I imagine Lizzie and Nancy are after the same thing I am. Poster paint, right?" she asked us.

I nodded, wondering what she needed poster paint for.

I soon found out.

"We're all working on booths for the school fair next Saturday," Samantha went on. "And I've volunteered to do the posters for the hallway, too."

"Very nice," Mr. MacDermott commented. "It's good to see students give time to their school."

I tried to keep my mouth shut, Diary, but I just couldn't help myself. "You're doing a booth?" I asked Samantha.

"Sure," she said. "I told Billy my idea at lunch today, and he loved it. I think it's going to be *fabulous!*"

So I'd been wrong. She hadn't been inviting Billy to a party; she'd been telling him about her *fabulous* idea. She was horning in on the fair.

I could feel Nancy poking me in the back. I knew she wanted to go, but I had to find out what Samantha's idea was. I'm not sure why. I guess I was hoping it would be dumb, and I could feel superior to her for once.

"Friendship bracelets," she said when I asked. "They're really popular, even with the little kids. Candace and Jessica and I are going to weave tons of them. And they'll be in the school colors, so everybody will want one."

"Claremont Elementary has school colors?" I asked.

"Sure it does." She gave me a pitying smile for my ignorance. "They're the same as the junior high's — green and gold. My father can get the material very cheaply, too, so we won't have to charge much at all. Ten or fifteen cents. It's going to be a very popular booth."

Grudgingly, I decided she was right. A friendship bracelet in the school colors would be a big seller. If any of the older kids showed up (and they probably would, now that Samantha had given the fair her blessing), they'd definitely buy one. The younger kids would, too, so they could be like the older ones; and their parents would like them because they weren't some cheap plastic item that would wind up in the garbage an hour later.

"What a dope," Nancy said when we left MacDermott's.

"I know," I agreed. "But the bracelets are a good idea, even though I hate to admit it."

"No, they're not," she said. "Samantha wants to turn the fair into a fashion show. I can't believe Billy really liked the idea."

"He's not in charge or anything." I felt like I had to defend him, even though I wished he'd told her it was a rotten idea. "His mom just asked him to try to get some volunteers."

"And Samantha Howard volunteered. Ha!" Nancy said. "I knew she'd be jealous after I told her Billy asked you personally. When was the last time any of her crowd went to the fair, anyway? I bet she hasn't been to one since second grade. She just wants to make Billy like her."

Nancy was probably right, I thought gloomily. Of course, Billy's one of the few boys in class who seems human to me, and I didn't think he'd fall madly in love with Samantha just because she'd volunteered for the fair.

But I couldn't help wishing Nancy hadn't said anything at all to Samantha about Billy asking me personally. Now Samantha was going to try to take over the whole thing, like she always does. I could just see her ordering everybody around, me included.

"Bracelets. What a dope," Nancy said again. "Fairs are supposed to be junky and corny. Our booth's going to be a much bigger hit that hers."

I didn't say so, but I have my doubts, Diary. I still think the bracelets are a great idea. And they're so simple. No writing a script or making puppets and backdrops. Just a few hours of weaving and bingo — you sit back and take in the money. And the praise.

But even worse, now that Samantha's doing a booth, all the most popular kids will come to the fair. They'll crowd around her, laughing and talking and acting cool. They won't come to The Klaremont Krazies, that's for sure.

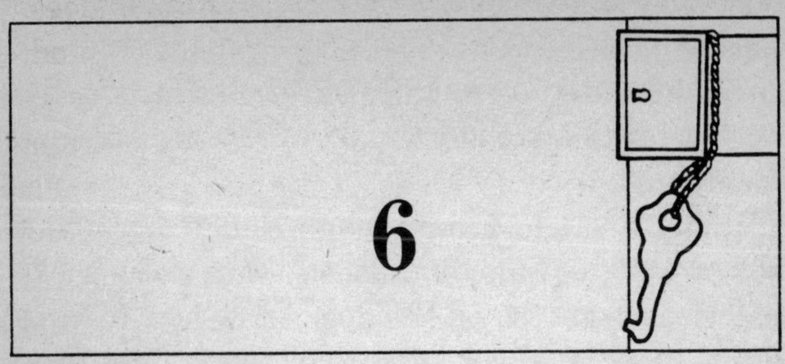

6

Dear Diary:

Saturday. Nancy's on the phone with her mother, and I'm in what she would call a pukey mood.

First of all, I'm still mad about Samantha and the fair. Mad isn't the right word, I guess. Bothered? Worried? Last night, after dinner, Nancy said I was obsessed. "Lizzie, you've got Samantha on the brain, you really do."

"I do not," I argued. "Just because I want our booth to be better than hers doesn't mean I'm obsessed." I rinsed a plate and handed it to Nancy, who put it in the dishwasher. "I want our booth to be better than anybody's."

"Well, the only one you've talked about is hers," Nancy argued back. "Billy said there are twenty booths. How come you're not worried about the other eighteen?"

"Okay, you're right," I admitted.

Nancy grinned and punched me on the arm. She

does that all the time. At least she didn't give me a noogie. "I knew it," she said.

"Anyway, who wants to sit around with some boring bracelets and gab all day? We're going to have fun."

I had to laugh. Even though Nancy acts about seven half the time, and doesn't care about looks and clothes and boys, she does know how to have fun. I wonder if part of growing up is forgetting that?

Anyway, I decided we'd make The Klaremont Krazies the best puppet show in the school's history, and I'd stop being obsessed with Samantha Howard.

"This is great, isn't it?" I said as I poured in the dishwasher powder.

"What, cleaning up?"

"Well, no. But doing it together, like roommates," I explained. "And not having to call each other later. We can make popcorn and work on the puppet show, and neither one of us will have to go home at a certain time, you know?"

Nancy nodded. "Even Oscar's settled in, like part of the family," she said.

I looked over at the cats. All three were hunched under the table, hoping for some more crumbs to fall.

I felt really good at that moment, Diary. My

best friend had just made me laugh, and our cats were buddies.

Then Adam came in, basketball in hand. "Hey, Nance," he said, trying to spin the ball on one fingertip. And failing. "Want to get beat again?"

"No." Nancy pushed her hair out of her eyes and grinned at him. "But I'd like to see you lose."

"First to score twenty?" Adam asked.

"Sure," Nancy said. "Two out of three?"

It sounded like some kind of code to me. But they obviously understood each other.

"You're on," Adam said. "Let's go."

So out they went, Diary, leaving me to sponge off the counters. All of a sudden, that nice, close, "roommate" feeling was gone, and I felt like Nancy had deserted me. I knew she hadn't, really. She was just acting like part of the family. But I thought we were going to work on the show. It's true, we hadn't made out any kind of formal schedule or anything, but I didn't think we needed to. We had lots to do, and I just naturally thought we'd start after dinner.

After I finished wiping the counters, I decided to work on the script until Nancy was finished, so I went up to my room. On the way up, I met Darcy.

"Where's Nancy?" she asked.

"Outside," I told her. "Playing basketball. Why?"

"I want her to read to me." Darcy held out a book. *Cloudy With a Chance of Meatballs.*

"You can read that," I said. "Why don't you read it to Rose, like Mom said?"

"Mom's washing Rose's hair," Darcy said. "She got honey in it. That kid is a real slob sometimes."

"Well, can't you wait?"

"I can, but I don't want to." By this time, we were in my room. Darcy had followed me there. "Want me to read it to you?" she asked.

I didn't, really, but it was only for a few minutes, so I said okay. Darcy settled down on my bed and read, and instead of writing, I started sorting through the bag of old clothes, looking for stuff that would work for hand puppets.

I guess I tuned her out, because suddenly I noticed she'd stopped reading.

"That was good, Darcy," I said quickly, pulling a red knit hat over my hand and wriggling it.

"Now you," she said, holding out *Charlotte's Web*. "We're on chapter two."

I hate to admit it, but I was trying to think of a way to turn her down, when Nancy came bounding into the room.

"Oh, did I miss the reading?" she said, collapsing on her chair and puffing out a big breath.

I said yes and Darcy said no.

"Darcy!" I said. "Nancy and I have to work on our puppet show."

"It'll just take a few minutes, Lizzie," Nancy said. "Besides, this is a good book."

"I know it's a good book," I told her. "I've read it dozens of times."

"Well, I haven't." Nancy's cheeks were pink and she fanned the air in front of her face. "Guess what? I beat Adam."

"Great," I muttered.

"Yeah, it was really fun." And without another word about the puppet show, or what *I* wanted to do, Nancy sat up, took the book from Darcy, and started reading.

I was annoyed, Diary, but I think I would have forgotten about it if it weren't for what happened later.

When the reading was over, Nancy and I wrote out the rest of the scenes for the show. We'd already talked about them on the way home and at dinner, so it didn't take too long.

When we finished, we were both starving, so we went downstairs to make popcorn. It was dark by now, and everybody except Josh (out with friends) and Dad (forgot some papers at the office) was gathered in the kitchen. Rose was there with her hair all shiny, eating some mysterious concoction from a Roth's Frozen Food container. Mom and Darcy were wrapping the birthday present Darcy's taking to Patty's party, and Adam was raiding the refrigerator.

"I thought you were going to the movies with Eric and staying over at his house," I said to him.

"I was," Adam said, biting into an apple. "But the jerk went to the mall and stayed too long and forgot to call home. It's the third time in two weeks he's done something like that, so his mom grounded him. For the whole weekend."

"Oh, too bad, " I said. "Mom, don't we have any microwave popcorn?"

"No, nobody put it on the list," she said. "If you want it, you'll have to make it the old-fashioned way."

"You can have some of this, Lizzie," Rose said, holding out her carton.

"What is it?"I asked suspiciously.

"Frozen yogurt."

"Yogurt? From Roth's?" Nancy said. "What's the catch?"

Adam laughed. "It's Frozen Yogurt with Garden Vegetables."

"I'll pass," Nancy said quickly.

"Have an apple," Adam suggested. "They're fresh, I guarantee it."

While Nancy and Adam munched on apples, and Rose polished off the last (I hope) of the vegetable yogurt, Mom gave me directions on making the popcorn.

"How's the puppet show coming?" she asked.

"Great," I said. I poured oil and popcorn into a

pan and turned on the burner. "We came up with this puppet we're calling Kid Detention. He's the terror of the teachers." I went on telling her about some of the scenes.

"It sounds wonderful, Lizzie," Mom said.

"Thanks. Now we've got to make the puppets and figure out how to build the stage," I said, shaking the pan. The corn was popping by this time, so I had to shout. "The puppets we can do after school, but we want to get the stage built this weekend, right, Nancy?"

No answer. I was making such a clatter, I just thought she couldn't hear me. But a moment later, when the popcorn was done, I turned around to ask her something, and she wasn't there. Darcy and Adam were gone, too, and Rose was on her way out.

"Where'd Nancy go?" I asked.

Mom put Darcy's present on top of the refrigerator, which is the safest place in the house. "I think I hear them in the family room," she said.

By then, I heard them, too. Actually, what I heard was the tinkly music of a Nintendo game. And when I went into the family room, there they were, gathered around the TV playing Super Mario Brothers II.

There's nothing wrong with playing Nintendo, of course. Even Josh, who pretends to be above it all, sneaks in a game once in a while. I don't happen to be crazy about it, but I play sometimes, when I'm home sick or while I'm waiting for the iron to heat up. What I mean is, I'll play when there's nothing better to do.

But there *was* something better to do last night. At least I thought there was. It was Friday. I'd just made popcorn. My best friend was over. Put those together and what do you get? You get sitting around in my room, talking and eating and gossiping and trying out new hairstyles. (This is the one fashion-type thing Nancy will agree to do.) *And*, you get some work done on the puppet show.

Nancy spent an entire hour and a half in front of the TV. She and Adam (Darcy got tired of it after a while) demolished the popcorn and traded corny jokes while I watched and got steamed.

Finally, I said, "It's ten o'clock. Don't you think we should figure out how we're going to make our puppet show stage?"

Nancy jumped a Zombie on the screen and didn't even turn around. "I thought we were going to do that tomorrow."

"Well, we are," I said. "But shouldn't we at least talk about it so we'll know what we're doing tomorrow?"

"Sure. Wait a minute, though." Nancy's eyes were glued to the television and she kept zapping Zombies as if the school fair were a month away instead of a week.

“Come on, Nancy!” I said.

“Lighten up, Lizzie,” Adam told me. “Gram and Ralph just bought a new washer and dryer and they still have the boxes. You can use those.”

“Great, they’ll be perfect. Right, Lizzie?” Nancy said. “What’s my score, Adam?”

Well, Diary, we finally did make it up to my room. And we did talk awhile before we finally went to sleep.

But when I got up this morning, I was still annoyed. Okay, so Adam solved the puppet stage problem. I should be happy and I am. But what if he hadn’t? Nancy seemed more interested in the stupid video game than in our booth. Even if she doesn’t care about competing with Samantha, the least she can do is care about doing a good job on The Klaremont Krazies. After all, she was the one who said how much fun it would be.

I don’t understand it. She doesn’t put her homework off, like I do. She’ll read to Darcy and help with the chores. Why isn’t she taking our puppet show seriously?

So that’s why I’m in a pukey mood, on Saturday of all days. Today, Nancy and I are supposed to work on the puppets until Gram and Ralph get here with the washer and dryer boxes. I hope she’s off the phone now, because I’m going down to remind her.

7

Dear Diary:

Sunday night. Gram's apartment again. And something ridiculous is happening with Nancy.

Yesterday, when I went down to find her, she was gone. In fact, everybody was gone and all I found were three notes on the refrigerator. One said that Josh had taken Darcy to her birthday party. The second one said Mom, Dad, and Rose had gone grocery shopping.

The third note said, "Lizzie. Out riding. Back fast. Nancy."

First of all, she wasn't back fast, Diary. Mom and Dad and I were putting groceries away when she finally strolled in. And she didn't come back alone, either. She came back with Adam.

"He let me ride his ten-speed," she said. "I think I know what to ask for for my birthday."

Not only is she the only sixth-grade girl I know who'd ask for a bike for her birthday, but she's the only one I know who'd go out riding instead of helping her best friend make puppets!

I was trying to think of a tactful way (I always try to be tactful) to tell her to stop goofing off, when Gram and Ralph arrived with the big boxes. So I decided to chew Nancy out later.

Gram and Ralph stayed for lunch, and that was the best part of the day. It felt like it used to, when Gram lived here.

When Gram's here, she makes me feel special. That's because I'm her favorite grandchild. She's never told me that, and I've never asked her. I just know it. I know she loves my brothers and sisters, too, of course, but she and I just have a closer connection. When she's around, I don't feel like the Middle Miletti Kid.

"Tell me all about everything," she said as we ate ham sandwiches and potato salad. "I need to catch up because Ralph and I have been up to our ears in work at the office."

Ralph smiled at her. "Betty just sold a house that nobody else could get anyone to look at," he said proudly. "It's run-down, to say the least. But she not only got a couple to look at it, she was able to make them see all its potential. They signed the papers yesterday."

That's what Gram does with me, I guess — makes me see my potential, especially when I'm feeling like a nerd. Next to me, I think Ralph is her biggest fan.

Gram laughed. "Now we'll be able to pay off

that new washer and dryer right away," she said. "Anyway, Lizzie, tell me about this puppet show you and Nancy are doing. It sounds very clever."

"It was Nancy's idea," I said. I wasn't being noble, Diary. I was still annoyed about the bike riding. But with Nancy right there, I felt like I had to give her credit.

I started describing the puppet show, and Nancy joined in. Pretty soon we were all laughing, and for a little while, I forgot about why I'd been grumpy.

But I remembered a few minutes later.

"So, Nancy, tell me," Gram said, smiling at her. They've always been good friends. "How's your mother doing on that job in Texas? Do you miss her?"

"She told me it's harder than she thought it would be, but she's really enjoying it," Nancy said. "I miss her some, but this is kind of like a second home. I'm having a great time."

Then, Diary, she went on and on about playing Nintendo and basketball and reading to Darcy and riding Adam's ten-speed. Not *once* did she mention me. Or the puppet show. Or the fact that it was now one-thirty in the afternoon and we hadn't done a single bit of work on it!

"Well, it sounds like it's working out just fine," Gram said. "I imagine you and Lizzie are staying up till all hours talking?"

"No," I said. I guess I said it kind of sharply, because Gram gave me a funny look. "I mean, not on school nights, anyway."

Nancy gave me a funny look, too, but I just went on eating.

When lunch was over, I pushed back my chair and stood up. "Nancy, maybe we'd better get those boxes off the top of Ralph's car," I said. "Once we get the stage built, we can start rehearsing."

"Good idea," she said. "But shouldn't we clean up in here first?"

"It's Adam's turn," I almost snapped.

After we lugged the boxes into the garage, we were just standing there looking at them, and Nancy said, "Lizzie, what's the matter with you? You almost bit my head off when I asked if we should clear the table."

"Well, I was kind of surprised," I said. "I mean, I never knew you were so conscientious about chores."

"I'm not. I hate chores," she said. "But Mom warned me not to act like this is a hotel. How come you're getting so mad just because I'm doing my share?"

"Because we've got to do *this!*" I said, pointing to the boxes. "The fair's a week away. The puppet show's not going to do itself! I just want to get this done in time," I said.

"Well, we will," she said. "This is going to be a cinch."

It wasn't exactly a cinch, but we were able to wrestle the boxes around and tape them together until they looked like a puppet show stage. It's a little lopsided, but we covered it with paper and painted all kinds of swirly designs on it, so maybe nobody will notice that it slopes. Across the top in big red letters are the words THE KLAREMONT KRAZIES.

"See?" Nancy said when we finished. "Now you can stop worrying."

We were eating dinner when Dad announced that he was leaving Monday on a business trip.

"This is a big one," he said, "and I won't be back until next Saturday."

"Are you selling Paisley Potatoes, Daddy?" Rose asked.

"Yes, Baby, and a lot of other new Roth products," he told her.

"Look out, America," Adam said.

"So," Daddy went on, ignoring Adam, "since I won't be here all week, I thought I might get a preview of that puppet show before I go." He smiled at Nancy and me. "How about it?"

"Sure," I said. "I mean, we have to rehearse anyway. It'll be good to have an audience. Just don't expect it to be perfect yet."

"Yet?" Josh asked. "Don't you mean 'ever'?"

"Very funny," I said. Then I turned to Nancy. "I guess we should do it alone a couple of times, huh? So we don't make fools of ourselves."

"Definitely," she said. "Right after I beat Adam at basketball again, we can bring the stage into the family room and practice."

Right after she beat Adam again. That's what she said, Diary. Well, I started to get mad again. But I wasn't going to say anything, not in front of everyone else. And while she was out in the driveway, leaping around in her paint-spattered sweatshirt and hair — *that's* when I started to wonder.

Did Nancy have a crush on Adam?

Of course, the first thing I thought was that it was ridiculous. I mean, Nancy doesn't like boys. Not *that way*, at least. Besides, Adam is my brother! She's known him as long as she's known me.

I told myself not to be dumb. I told myself she liked Adam and she was treating him like a buddy. But she'd never done that before. And Adam is thirteen. You don't pal around with a boy two years older than you are unless you have a crush on him. I know I'm not an expert, but I don't think you do, anyway.

I was dying to ask her, but I knew I couldn't

do that. Even if it was true, she'd never admit it. She'd get all huffy and red in the face and accuse me of having boys on the brain.

So I kept my mouth shut and watched.

Here's what happened: Nancy and Adam played basketball after dinner. Then Nancy and I rehearsed the puppet show alone in the family room. We still didn't have puppets, so we used socks. The whole thing went pretty well, but we decided not to show it to Dad until today.

After that, everybody but Josh (who went to a big party) played Pictionary. It was fun for a while, but I kept waiting for Nancy to suggest that we go hang out in my room. That's what we usually do. But she didn't. She and Adam would have played all night, I think. It was the rest of us who finally called it quits.

Now for this morning: We were eating a big Sunday breakfast and it went like this:

Nancy (starting on her third stack of pancakes): I'm going to feel like a blimp when I'm done with this.

Me (also on my third stack): I already do.

Adam (to me): You look like one, too.

Nancy (after laughing too loud at Adam's junior-high wit): I think I'll bike over to the nature preserve. It's a great day and I haven't been there in a while. Want to come, Lizzie?

Me: I thought we were going to start making the puppets today.

Nancy: We are. But the preserve's not that far, and besides, the ride will sort of help us digest all this food.

Adam: What's at the nature preserve?

Nancy: Birds. Lots of them. And maybe some rare ones, if I'm lucky.

Me: I think I'll wash my hair instead. I've still got paint in it.

Adam: Oh, is that paint? I thought you'd gone punk and streaked it with green.

Me: Ha, ha. Anyway, I can bend a lot in the shower and digest breakfast at the same time.

Nancy (still laughing at Adam's not-so-clever remark): Well, I'm going to take a ride over there. Do you want to come, Adam?

Adam: Sure, why not?

That convinced me, Diary. It might have sounded very casual and "who cares?", but it wasn't. I know Nancy. She doesn't invite just anybody to go bird-watching with her. And I know she's never invited a boy.

Like I said, it's ridiculous. But it might be kind of interesting if it weren't for the puppet show. I'm counting on her for that, and she knows it. She couldn't have picked a worse time to discover a boy.

8

Dear Diary:

It's Monday and I should be doing my homework now, but I don't want to. I want to talk. I'm glad I have you, Diary.

It's true that the nature preserve isn't that far away, but it's not exactly next door, either. Nancy and Adam were gone for three hours yesterday!

"I don't believe this," I said, after two hours had gone by. "If she doesn't hurry and get back, we'll never be able to give Dad his preview."

"It's only two-thirty, Lizzie," Mom pointed out calmly. "I imagine you'll have plenty of time."

I'd just finished washing my hair and had come down to the kitchen to see if they were back yet. Nobody else was in sight, and Mom was drinking iced tea and reading the travel section of the Sunday paper. Do you suppose she dreams of escaping the Miletti Fun House? I know she enjoys having time to herself, even three minutes, but I was too grumpy to leave her in peace.

"It's only two-thirty *now*," I said. "Who knows

what time it'll be when she gets back?"

"Mmm." Mom turned a page. "Maybe Nancy spotted a rare bird. It's nice having her stay with us, isn't it? I think everybody's enjoying it. She's a big help, too."

"I could use her help right now," I said. "We've got twelve puppets to make and we haven't even started."

Mom looked up from the paper. "Well, Lizzie, why don't you get started by yourself now? Then when Nancy comes back you'll be that much farther along."

Mom was being reasonable, but that wasn't the point. The point is this is a *joint* project. As in "together." If I'd wanted to do it by myself, I wouldn't have asked Nancy in the first place. And I sure wouldn't have asked her if I'd known she was going to turn out to be such a busy roommate.

By the time Nancy and Adam got back, I had one puppet sort of halfway put together. The head was a problem. I was using a softball and it was too heavy. There also wasn't any place for my fingers. Nancy came into the room, took one look at it, and said, "The head flops."

"I know it flops," I told her. I'd decided not to ask how the bird-watching went. "At least it's *got* a head."

"Yeah, but it's no good," she said.

I tried gritting my teeth, but I couldn't keep

from saying, "Do you have a better idea?"

Nancy must really be crazy about Adam, because she didn't even seem to notice how sarcastic I sounded.

"I think I do," she said. "Adam and I were just putting our bikes in the garage and I saw this box of Styrofoam balls. They're a little bit bigger than that softball, and that's even better. The face will show more."

Reluctantly, I went out to the garage with her. Just as reluctantly, I had to admit she was right. The Styrofoam balls were perfect. They were left over from one Christmas when we stuck stars and glitter on them for decorations. But I really hate it when somebody who's been out having fun while you do all the dirty work comes along and points out what you've done wrong.

We didn't make any puppets then, though. Dad had things to do and didn't want to miss the preview, so we used socks again. Everybody but Josh watched.

Nancy was good, using all kinds of different voices and really getting into it, but I didn't feel like complimenting her.

Adam did, though. I was getting something for us to drink when he came into the kitchen and said, "Hey, the show's not bad."

"Thanks."

"Of course, the humor's a little juvenile."

"Adam," I said, "it's mainly for kids Darcy's age. She laughed a lot, and so did Rose. Anyway, I heard you and Dad laughing a lot, too."

He downed a glass of juice. "Well, Nancy was really funny," he said.

"Mmm."

"The nature preserve was kinda neat," he said. "Nancy's okay, you know?" Then he slugged me on the shoulder and left.

Oh, great, I thought. If Adam thinks Nancy's okay, she'll know it, and she'll hang out with him even more. Leaving me holding the Styrofoam balls!

So here it is, Monday night, and I'm sitting here staring at two extremely weird-looking puppets on my bed. One is made out of an old black sweater that used to be Dad's. Its head is the Styrofoam ball with a black felt hat and black yarn eyebrows glued to it and a big frown painted on it. This is supposed to be the principal. No matter how much I squint my eyes and tilt my head, it still looks like a Styrofoam ball with an old sweater attached to it.

I made it, and it isn't going to win any prizes, that's for sure. But it's finished.

The other one is supposed to be a student. Darcy let Nancy have one of her old rag dolls for this one. Nancy pulled some of the stuffing out so there'd be a place for her hand, and it already has stringy yellow yarn for hair. But it needs clothes.

Nancy decided to cut up some old jeans and a T-shirt for it. But she hasn't done it yet.

She isn't goofing off with Adam (not now, anyway). She had to go to her reading tutor after school, so Josh drove her there. She said she'd finish the puppet when she got back, after she did her homework. But I have my doubts.

One-and-a-half puppets, Diary. That's what we have, with four days to go until the fair.

I was going to tell her on the way to school this morning that we'd better hurry and get them done, and I was trying to decide if I should be tactful or just come right out and yell at her, when Adam started walking with us.

Even though Claremont Junior High is right next to the elementary school, Adam would usually rather catch the plague than be seen with two sixth-grade girls. But there he was, and before I could even mention the puppets, he and Nancy were gabbing away about birds and bikes and skateboards. I trailed along, feeling like a third wheel and wondering how Nancy could do this to me.

If I wasn't so mad at Nancy, I might have enjoyed what happened next.

We had just passed Samantha's house when we noticed her and Candace a few yards ahead of us.

Well, *I* noticed. Nancy was too busy talking about a pair of binoculars she wants, and Adam has never noticed Samantha.

Adam said something and Nancy laughed. Loudly. So loudly that Samantha and Candace turned around to see who would be uncool enough to shriek in public.

Diary, you should have seen the look on Samantha Howard's face! After she'd gone to so much sneaky trouble to try to get Adam to notice her, and after she'd failed miserably, here he was walking to school with Nancy Underpeace! The girl who wears Snoopy sweatshirts and checkered sneakers. The girl who still climbs trees and thinks water balloons are hilariously funny. The girl who couldn't care less about being cool was walking with the boy who doesn't even know super-cool Samantha is alive!

Later, after homeroom, while Nancy was still getting her books together, Samantha waited for me in the hall.

"I just wanted to make sure your booth is going to be ready for Saturday, Lizzie," she said. "Billy's mother asked me to check with everyone."

Ha. Samantha probably volunteered. I bet she just wanted to make Billy's mother like her, so she'd say nice things about her to Billy. "Well, you can tell her it'll be ready," I said, crossing my fingers that it would. "Nancy and I even gave a private showing over the weekend and it was a big hit."

"Oh. That's nice." Samantha glanced into homeroom. "Uh, Lizzie," she said. "I noticed your brother walking with Nancy this morning."

"That's right," I said.

"Are they . . ." Samantha lowered her voice. "I mean, he doesn't actually *like* her, does he?"

What a jerk, I thought. Talking about Nancy as if no boy in the world could possibly like her. Here was my chance to really get back at Samantha and tell her, yes, Adam is madly in love with Nancy Underpeace.

"Well, Samantha." I paused.

"Well, what?" She flipped her perfect hair back impatiently.

"I'm just not sure what the situation is," I told her.

And that's all I said. I didn't deny it, but I was just too annoyed with Nancy at the moment to stick up for her or to humiliate Samantha. When I didn't take my chance to do that, I knew the situation was serious.

The only thing to do is talk to Nancy.

Well, Diary, I did. Talk to Nancy, I mean. I was determined to be calm and not yell or call her names, but it didn't work out that way. It never does, it seems.

Nancy's asleep now in my totally dark room and I'm up in the attic apartment again. I just finished crying. I waited until I got up here, but then I really let go!

After dinner tonight we made four more puppets (six more to go) and then Nancy went down to the kitchen to get us something to nibble on. I kept working while I waited. And waited. And waited.

"What did you do?" I asked when she finally came back with some juice and peanut-butter sandwiches. "Pick the oranges from the trees or something?"

"Sorry," she said, biting into a sandwich. "Darcy asked me to read to her. We're still on *Charlotte's Web* and it was a really long chapter."

I was all ready to say something, but she went right on, "And then Adam was in the kitchen and we just joked around for a while."

"For a while?" I said.

"Yeah, he's pretty funny sometimes."

"For a *while?*" I said again. "Nancy, you were down there for forty-five minutes! We have to get these puppets done!"

Nancy swallowed a big bite of sandwich and looked at me. "Promise you won't get mad?" she said.

"I'm already mad."

"Then don't get any madder, okay?" she asked.

"But you're really starting to act like a jerk about this puppet show, Lizzie."

Now I know what it means to be speechless, because when I opened my mouth, nothing came out. It didn't last more than ten seconds, though. "What do you mean, I'm acting like a jerk?"

"You're just making it work, work, work," she said. " 'Hurry up, Nancy, we've got to get done.' " She was actually imitating my voice! And she was pretty good at it, which made me even madder. " 'Come on, Nancy, let's work on the puppet show instead of hanging out for ten minutes like regular kids.' It's no fun, Lizzie."

"Ten minutes? Ha!" I said. "It's more like ten hours. You're always finding something else to do." I would have tried imitating *her* voice, but I'm not that good at it. "You have to read with Darcy or help with the chores. *Or*," I said, "you hang out with Adam, who happens to be much too old for you, Nancy Underpeace!"

Now Nancy was speechless. Her face started to get pink and her eyes got real wide.

"I know you like him," I said. "But it's the most ridiculous thing I ever heard of."

Nancy was glaring at me and I thought she was going to yell. But then she shook her head and took another bite of her sandwich. How she can eat when we're fighting is one of life's unsolved mysteries. "You know what?" she said with her mouth full.

"What?"

"You're jealous, that's all."

I tossed down my puppet and laughed. "That's really dumb, Nancy. Adam is my brother. How could I be jealous about him?"

"I don't mean Adam," she said. "I mean jealous of me. Because I like to have fun. You're so worried about being cool, and doing better than Samantha at the fair, and impressing Billy, that you don't have any fun. And you don't want anybody else to have any, either."

At that moment, Diary, I wished that Nancy had never become my roommate.

P.S.: I forgot the only good news I have — I got a C on the pop quiz.

9

Dear Diary:

When Nancy came to stay with us, I didn't think I'd have much time to write in you, Diary. I was sure the two of us would be up late talking every night, like we do when we sleep over at each other's houses, and that I'd have to wait until the two weeks were over, and then write a super-long entry, telling how much fun we had. Instead, I'm writing almost every day, and I'm not writing about fun, am I?

After our argument last night, I wasn't even sure Nancy and I would be speaking to each other. Well, we are, but you couldn't call it friendly.

I overslept this morning, and it was Nancy who got me up. Nancy was jiggling my bed. With her foot. She had one bare foot on the mattress and she kept jabbing at it with her extremely long toes.

"Why are you doing that?" I mumbled. I was

still too groggy to remember we were mad at each other.

"Your mom asked me to get you up," she said. "We have to leave in twenty minutes. I guess you didn't hear your alarm."

I panicked and threw back the covers. "Why didn't you wake me?" I cried.

"I was downstairs getting something to eat," she said. "I just figured you'd wake up when your alarm went off."

Still in a panic, I rushed to the bathroom and washed up. When I got back to my room, Nancy was on the floor, pulling on her socks and shoes. Her old shoes. For some reason that old pair of shoes really got on my nerves this morning. Maybe because I was awake enough by then to remember our argument, so it didn't take much to set me off.

"When are you going to break in your new ones?" I asked, as I pulled a blue-and-green striped polo shirt out of a pile of clean stuff I hadn't put away yet.

"When I feel like it," she said, calmly tying her laces.

"Well," I said sarcastically, "if you like Adam, you ought to start dressing nicer."

"For your information," Nancy said, "I do not happen to 'like' Adam. But if I did, I'd think you'd be happy. After all, you're always telling me I should start changing and growing up."

I zipped up my blue cotton skirt and started shoving things into my bookbag. "I don't believe you," I told her. "I think you do like him and you're embarrassed to say so. But I really don't care. I just wish you'd waited until we finished the puppet show before you decided to grow up."

Nancy picked up *her* bookbag (her old one, with dinosaurs on it) and walked to the door. "Don't worry about the puppet show," she said. "I'll help you finish it if it's the last thing I do. But I sure won't have fun doing it."

Things didn't get much better after that, Diary. It's very confusing. She's my roommate for two weeks and I thought we'd be talking and working together all the time. I really don't understand it. What's so wrong about wanting her to spend more time working with me on the show?

And I know she's lying about Adam. He walked with us again this morning and Nancy talked to him the whole time. I was beginning to wonder if maybe Adam liked her, too. *Liked* her, I mean. But Adam was just treating her like another guy, I decided.

Adam had just left us and was walking on toward the junior high, when Samantha, Candace, and Jessica came strolling up behind us.

"Well, Nancy," Samantha said. She completely ignored me. "I see you finally discovered that boys exist."

"Took you long enough," Jessica said.

Candace smirked.

I guess Samantha had decided that if she couldn't get Adam interested in her, she'd make fun of the whole situation. I waited to see what Nancy would do. If she was still the same old Nancy, she'd say something like "stick it in your ear," or "blow it out your nose," or even just "get lost."

Instead, she smiled at them. She didn't say a word, just smiled, a funny little smile, like she was happy and embarrassed at the same time. Then she walked into the school.

"I don't get it," I said as we headed for homeroom. "How could you let them talk to you like that?"

"I just don't care what they think," Nancy said. Then, she gave *me* that funny little smile!

So, you see, she wasn't telling the truth about not liking Adam.

In homeroom, Ms. Basley brought up a sore subject — the fair. Of course, she didn't know it was a sore subject. She was very enthusiastic and started out by asking, "Is everyone looking forward to the school fair? I hope we get a really good turnout!"

"The fair?" Donald Harrington said. "Pardon me while I fall asleep."

Like I said, not many sixth-graders go to it, and most of the kids yawned loudly. But then Samantha stuck her hand up. "I'd just like to say that the school fair is a very worthy event," she said.

"Worthy of what?" somebody asked.

"She means 'worthwhile,' I think," Robert said.

Samantha frowned at him. "Whatever," she said. "Anyway, the money we make is going to help buy new library books, so it's for a good cause. I'm helping Mrs. Watts organize it *and* I'm doing a booth myself."

"That's wonderful, Samantha," Ms. Basley beamed. She's really big on organization and school spirit. "What is your booth going to be?"

"This." Samantha pulled out a bracelet braided in green and gold. "Friendship bracelets," she said proudly. "I think they'll be really popular, and I hope everyone turns out and buys one for the good of the Claremont Elementary School library."

What a speech, Diary! As usual, Samantha was trying to take charge and make herself the most important person around. And it seemed to be working. Most of the girls and even one or two of the boys thought the bracelet was cool. I liked it, too, I hate to admit.

Samantha was totally thrilled. "I'm sure you've

all seen the posters I did for the halls," she said. "There are going to be twenty booths and the whole thing is going to be really fun."

"I never read the hall posters," Donald said. "I hope there's something else to do there besides buy jewelry."

"Of course there is," Ms. Basley said. "There's going to be a beanbag toss and clown makeup and a cakewalk, and . . . oh, just a lot of fun things."

"Lizzie and Nancy are doing a puppet show," Billy Watts said.

I think Billy was trying to be nice, Diary. He probably didn't want Nancy and me to feel left out. But I wish he hadn't said it, because Ms. Basley got even more enthusiastic and insisted that Nancy and I tell everybody about the show.

Nancy and I glanced at each other and I finally said, "It's called 'The Klaremont Krazies.' "

"It's a puppet show," Nancy said. She sounded very grim.

"We already know that," Polly said. "What's the plot?"

"It doesn't have one," I said, sounding just as grim. "It's just a bunch of different scenes."

"You know — crazy, silly," Nancy said in a monotone. "Like an old Punch and Judy show."

"And you two collaborated on this?" Ms. Basley looked a little confused, like why weren't we more excited about it?

"Yep," Nancy told her.

"Uh-huh," I agreed.

"What's with you guys?" Billy asked as we left Ms. Basley's class. "When you talked about the puppet show, you made it sound about as much fun as a visit to the dentist."

"That's what it's starting to feel like," Nancy said.

"Come on, Nancy!" I cried. "Just because I think we could work a little harder on it, you don't have to make me sound like a slave driver."

"Uh-oh," Billy said. "Maybe I shouldn't have asked."

I could feel my eyes start to fill up. Was I going to cry, right there in the hall, right in front of Billy Watts?

Fortunately, Donald Harrington saved me. He came marching down the hall behind us, making a disgusting burping sound with every step. So I blinked real fast a few times and took a deep breath. "Donald Harrington!" I yelled. "When are you going to join the human race?"

Donald stuck his fingers in his mouth and stretched his cheeks real wide and wiggled his tongue at me as he marched on by. I didn't feel great, but I felt a little better. At least I hadn't cried.

Now, Diary, I'm in my room. I just finished my

homework. So did Nancy, except she did hers in the kitchen. She's still down there, making puppets. I made two up here. Alone. She was right about it not being fun.

But it's her fault, isn't it?

10

Dear Diary:

It's Wednesday night, and by now, you can guess where I am. Up in Gram's apartment. I'm beginning to think I should move up here permanently.

I went shopping today after school. After everything I've been saying, I know I should have gone right home and finished the puppets, but I just couldn't do it. I had to get away by myself. I guess most people wouldn't pick a mall to get away in, but I can feel alone there even when it's packed. I called home so Mom would know, and she said okay, but for us not to stay too long. She assumed Nancy was going with me, and I didn't tell her she wasn't.

Nancy and I were still speaking (barely), but when I told her I was going to the mall, she just said, "Oh. I'm going to my house and water the plants again. See you later."

We arrived home at the same time, and I was kind of surprised.

"Are you just getting back from your house?" I asked.

"Yep."

She'd been there for an hour and a half, Diary. You'd think she had a jungle to take care of, instead of a few little houseplants. I wondered if maybe Nancy had wanted to be alone, too. And that made me sad. We'd been so excited at being able to spend all our time together, and now we were finding reasons to be apart.

I almost said something, but before I could decide how to say it without getting in another argument, we were in the house. And the minute we walked in the door, we knew something bad had happened.

The first thing we heard was Rose crying. She kept saying "It's okay, Mommy. It's okay, Mommy," in between the sobs.

Darcy hadn't seen us come in. She was standing at the basement door and she wasn't crying, but her voice was real quivery. "I'll call an ambulance," she said. "I know what to say. I even know the number."

Ambulance? Nancy and I both dropped our books and ran over to Darcy.

"What happened?" I cried. "Who's sick?"

Darcy pointed, and we looked down the basement stairs. Mom was at the bottom, half sitting, half lying on the floor. A huge pile of laundry was scattered around her. Her face was pale and she had her bottom lip between her teeth. Rose was squatting beside her, patting her shoulder.

"Mom!" I hustled down the stairs, with Nancy and Darcy right behind me. "What happened? What happened?"

"It's all right, Lizzie, everybody," Mom said. "Really, there's no need to panic. But I'm afraid I do need to go to the hospital."

At that, Rose sobbed loudly and Darcy did start crying.

"Wait, wait, don't panic," Mom said again. She even laughed a little. "Rosie, Darcy, all I did was twist my ankle. I'm going to be fine. But I'll need an X ray to make sure it's not broken, and they can only do that in a hospital. Okay?"

"Okay," Darcy quivered.

Rose sniffed and wiped her nose on the shoulder of her T-shirt.

"How did it happen, Mrs. Miletti?" Nancy asked.

"A laundry basket, what else?" Mom said, shaking her head. "After all the times I've told everybody not to leave a basket at the top of the stairs, *I* was the one who did it."

"You mean you fell all the way down the stairs?" I cried. "What about your head?"

"I need to have it examined for leaving the stupid basket in the way, but otherwise it's all right," Mom said. "I caught my heel in the basket up at the top, but I managed to keep my balance until the next to last step. I came down on it off balance, and my ankle just twisted in the opposite direction from the way I was going."

Darcy had stopped crying by now. "I'll go call the ambulance."

"No, Darcy, honey, don't do that," Mom said. "I really don't need one. Josh can drive me to the hospital."

"But Josh isn't here," Darcy said.

"I can wait," Mom told her.

"Mom, do you want us to help you up the stairs?" I asked.

"Thanks, Lizzie, but let's just wait. I don't want to move until I have to."

Josh didn't get home for another hour, and by then the house was like the Red Cross. I made Mom some tea and took it down to her. Nancy picked up the laundry and put it away, then brought her a peanut-butter sandwich. Darcy kept running up and down with quilts and pillows, and Rose brought down a box of Kleenex and her favorite stuffed bear. Mom didn't need them, but Rose sure did.

Adam came home in the middle of all our scurrying around and offered to drive the car himself.

"I don't think the police would mind, not when they hear the reason," he said.

"They might not, but *I* would," Mom laughed. "No, Adam, thank you, but you'll have to wait until you're sixteen, like everybody else."

Well, Josh finally got home and we got Mom up the stairs and into the car. Everybody wanted to go, of course.

"It'll be like a zoo if we all go," Josh complained. "Besides, we won't all fit."

"Let Rose and Darcy come so they'll know what it's all about," Mom said. "Lizzie, Adam, Nancy, you get things organized and start dinner, okay?"

I thought maybe with what happened, Nancy and I would sort of forget about our own problems. And we did, but it only lasted a few minutes.

"That was kind of scary, wasn't it?" Nancy said. She was ripping up lettuce for a salad.

I took a meat loaf (homemade, not Roth's) out of the freezer and put it in the oven. "It was awful," I agreed. "Imagine if she *had* hit her head. I guess we take Mom for granted a lot. Maybe we won't after this."

"Come on, you guys," Adam said as he twisted a tie around a garbage bag. "Don't get all mopey. She twisted her ankle, that's all."

"We're not being mopey," I said. "We were just worried. So were you. I could tell, Adam Miletti."

Adam blushed a little. "Okay, but I'm not anymore." He hefted the garbage bag like a Santa sack. "I'll be out shooting baskets now that the big scare is over. Nance, you want to play?"

I didn't say a word, Diary. I wanted to, naturally. But I managed to keep my lips buttoned.

"I'd like to, but I can't," Nancy said.

I breathed a silent sigh of relief.

"I have to do my homework," she said. "And then I have to help finish the puppets."

It wasn't *what* she said, Diary. It was the *way* she said it, like maybe if she tried real hard, she could stand the idea of finishing the puppets. Like it was a real chore.

I still didn't say anything, though. With Mom hurt and all, the last thing the Miletti house needed was a fight. I just set the table and went upstairs. I guess Nancy finished her puppet in the family room, because later, when Mom and the others got home, I saw it sitting on top of our laundry-box stage.

Mom's ankle *was* broken, after all. She thumped into the house on crutches, with her foot in a cast. But she was smiling. She'd seen a doctor there that she used to work with when she was a nurse, and they caught up on each other's lives.

Darcy and Rose didn't look worried anymore, either. They'd both gotten ice-cream cups in the hospital cafeteria and balloons in the gift shop, and they seemed to think the whole thing had been an exciting adventure.

"This looks good!" Mom exclaimed when we sat down to eat. "Thanks, Lizzie, Nancy."

"Don't forget yours truly," Adam reminded her. "I took out the garbage."

Mom reached over and tried to ruffle his hair, but he ducked away. Things seemed back to normal.

Dad called during dinner, and so did Gram. Mom insisted that she be the one to tell them what happened, so they wouldn't worry.

After Gram's call, she said, "Mother wanted to know if she should come stay here, just until Dad gets back, but I told her no."

"Why?" Darcy asked. "She and Ralph could both come. It would be fun."

"Yes, but they have busy lives of their own," Mom told her. "And this isn't an emergency. It *is* an inconvenience, though." She looked around the table. "It's going to mean extra chore duty for everyone, even when Dad does get back."

"No problem," Josh said. "Maybe I should make up a list."

"Go ahead," Adam told him. "Just don't expect anybody to read it."

"What's wrong with a list?" Darcy asked. I think she and Josh have a lot in common, Diary. "I like lists."

"This isn't the army, Josh," I said. "We can do extra chores without checking some dumb list."

"Please," Mom said. "Work it out any way you like, but just make sure the chores get done. And please," she added, looking tired all of a sudden, "try to cooperate."

We were wonderful, Diary, at least after dinner. Nancy did some more laundry. Josh helped Mom up to bed, and then he bundled up about three months' worth of newspapers that he'd been putting off doing. Adam and I cleaned up the kitchen, and Darcy helped Rose with her bath. Nancy also read to Darcy. Again.

As far as I know, nobody argued or bickered with anybody else. Until later.

Nancy and I were in bed. I had my little light on because I was looking at a clothes catalogue I'd gotten at the mall. I didn't buy a single thing when I was there, except a Coke. The catalogue had some great sweaters in it, and I was thinking about saving my money for one in particular — a green one with a pattern of fall-colored leaves knitted into it. Even though Nancy isn't interested in clothes for herself, in normal times, I would have shown her the picture and asked her opinion. But these aren't normal times, so I didn't.

After a while, I had trouble keeping my eyes open. Maybe it was Mom's accident — you get tense and then when it's all over, you feel like you've just finished gym class. I could feel the catalogue slipping out of my hands, and before I knew it, I fell asleep. I don't know what woke me, but when my eyes popped open, the room was completely dark. Nancy must have turned off the light. I kept staring where I knew the window was, but it must have gotten cloudy, because I couldn't see a thing.

I reached up and snapped on the lamp, and snuggled back into my pillow.

In a few minutes, I heard Nancy start to toss around. Then she groaned. "Oh, Lizzie, could you please shut that off? I can't sleep with it on."

I sighed, but I shut it off. Then *I* started tossing around. "I can't sleep with it off," I finally said. "I want some light tonight."

This time, Nancy sighed. "Okay, okay," she said in a martyred tone. Then she pulled her pillow over her head.

I stomped out of the room and got a towel, like before. After I'd draped it over the lamp, I snapped it on and said, "See if this is all right."

She pushed the pillow off her head, and after a few minutes, I thought she was asleep. Her breathing was slow and easy, anyway. And I was worried about the towel. What if it got so hot it caught fire? With this lamp, I knew it would take a long time, but still, it could happen, couldn't it?

Slowly, silently, I slid the towel off.

"Uunngghh!"

"Come on, Nancy," I said, "it's not the sun! It's a puny little lamp!"

"I can't help it!" she said. "I can't sleep with that dumb thing on! Anyway, if it's so little, how come it makes you feel safer?"

"That's not why I want it," I said. "I just like to know where I am if I wake up in the middle of the night, that's all."

"How come you never needed a night-light any of the other times I've slept over?" she asked.

"I don't know," I said. "How come I never knew you had to have it pitch-dark? And why didn't I know you were so neat?"

"Neat?" she cried. "What's that got to do with your night-light?"

"Stop calling it a night-light!" I yelled. "And you are neat. You actually fold your clothes and put them in drawers!"

"That's not neat, that's normal."

"It's disgusting," I said. "Disgustingly neat!"

Suddenly Josh shouted up the stairs, "Would you guys hold it down? I've got a chemistry test tomorrow!"

Then Darcy hollered, "Yeah. Besides, you're going to wake Mom. And the neighbors. I'd be soooo embarrassed!"

Nancy and I both puffed out big breaths of air. "Well, I'm going to sleep," Nancy said huffily. She flopped back down, pulling the covers *and* the pillow over her head.

But I couldn't sleep, even with the light, Diary. So I turned it off and came up here.

Now's the time I really wish Gram were still living with us. I know she couldn't do anything about Nancy, but at least she'd listen to me. And she'd understand, I know she would. I'm trying to decide whether to go see her, or whether to just hang on until Monday, when Mrs. Underpeace gets back and Nancy goes home.

That last sentence makes me want to cry. I never thought I'd look forward to seeing my best friend leave.

11

Dear Diary:

I was right about the clouds last night. When I got up this morning, it was raining. It rained the entire day. Sometimes I like it, especially a warm rain in the summer, or when I'm riding in the car. I like the sound of it on the car roof, like grains of rice spilling all over a countertop.

But today it wasn't warm, and besides, my hair frizzed out like an exploded Brillo pad. Mom told me once that my hair was straight as a stick until I turned three. I wonder if I went through some major trauma back then that left me with these impossible curls.

Adam did not walk to school with us today. He had to get to the junior high early for basketball practice, I think. I'm not sure his absence was good or bad. I certainly didn't miss him, but without him, conversation between Nancy and me was not exactly lively.

Me: I guess we'd better start figuring out how we're going to get the puppet stage to school.

Nancy: Right.

Nancy (after half a block): It's light. We can carry it. That'll be easier than tying it to the top of a car.

Me: Right.

Me (after another halfblock): The fair starts at ten-thirty. We should probably get there by nine, so we can set up and stuff.

Nancy: Okay.

One good thing about Adam not being with us, Diary: If Nancy wants to impress him, she sure wouldn't have this morning. I was wearing my poncho, but Nancy hadn't brought hers to our house, and it was too late to stop and get it. At first, she was just going to wear that awful gray sweatshirt with the hood up, but Mom insisted it was raining too hard. She made us hunt through those bags of old clothes until we found Josh's old yellow rain slicker.

Josh must have worn it before he got tall, because the sleeves came up almost to Nancy's elbows and the hem hit her way above the knees. I would have put up a fight about wearing it, but Nancy — being Nancy — loved it. "It's just like the one I had in kindergarten," she said, after putting it on in the kitchen.

"That may have been the last time Josh wore it," Mom laughed.

Darcy looked at it and cocked her head to one

side. “It’s cute,” she finally announced.

Darcy would think it was cute if Nancy decided to go to school in her pajamas. Ever since they became “Partners in Reading,” Darcy thinks everything Nancy says or does is perfect.

You see what this situation is doing to me? Now I’m criticizing my little sister just because she likes my supposed best friend.

I wondered how the cool group at school would react to such an uncool piece of clothing. And to the fact that Adam wasn’t with us this morning.

I found out as soon as we got to the front doors. The Snob Queen and her two Princesses emerged from Samantha’s father’s car just as Nancy and I were sprinting up the front walk.

The three of them came hurrying in behind us, squealing about what the rain was doing to their hair. Just inside the doors, Nancy and I stopped to shake off our raincoats. Ms. Basley can’t stand puddles.

“Oh, Lizzie,” Samantha said, “I’m glad to see you.”

“You are?”

“I need to give you your assigned spot at the fair.”

“Assigned spot?” I said. I noticed Samantha was talking to me, but she was looking at Nancy, who still didn’t have her slicker all the way off. “Well,” I said, “I don’t know where we’ve been *assigned*, but since it's a puppet show, I think we're going to need the little stage at the end of the cafeteria."

"What do you need a stage for?" Candace asked. *She* was looking at Nancy, too, and so was Jessica.

"Because nobody would be able to hear us if we're out in the middle of the cafeteria with all the other booths," I said. "If we're on the stage, behind the curtain, it'll be quieter. Kids can buy their tickets and we'll do the show for . . . I don't know . . . twenty at a time."

"Hmmm," Samantha said, still keeping an eye on Nancy. "Well, I had you over by the tray return."

"That's ridiculous," I told her. "It's by the doors, too. We'd have to scream our heads off to be heard."

"Hmmm," she said again. Then she sighed, very dramatically. "Well, I don't know. I'll have to talk to Billy's mother, I guess. I helped her make out the booth assignments. She'll have to tell me if it's okay."

I was about to say that we were going to do the puppet show on the stage, no matter *where* she'd already assigned us, but the bell rang then and we all headed for classes.

Looking back, I saw that The Too Cool Trio had their heads together and their eyes on Nancy. They hadn't spoken to her, but they sure had watched her. Maybe they were trying to decide if yellow rain slickers four sizes too small were what junior-high guys liked.

If things had been normal between me and Nancy, we could have had a big laugh about that. But I didn't have time to feel too sad just then; first I had to take care of where our booth was going to be.

Right after English, I waylaid Billy in the hall. Nancy obviously didn't care about the problem, and besides, she'd stayed behind to discuss an essay with Mr. Rice. Ever since he learned about her dyslexia, he's been really helpful by letting her bring a lot of her work in a day late, instead of having to write it right there in class.

"Billy," I said, "you've got to do me a favor."

"Okay. If I can," he said.

I quickly explained about our "assigned spot." "It'll be a disaster by the tray return," I said. "But Samantha's got this idea that your mother won't want us to use the stage. She said she'd ask her, but — "

Billy interrupted with a funny little laugh. "I bet she will," he said. "She's been calling my mom every night, almost. I don't know why and neither does Mom."

I was pretty sure I knew why, Diary. Samantha was hoping Billy would answer so she could talk to him. Then she'd be able to mention it in school. It's the kind of thing Samantha would do. To be honest, it's the kind of thing I've *thought* about doing (the calling part, anyway), but I never had a good enough reason. Or enough nerve.

"Anyway," Billy went on, "my mother said Samantha's been helpful, but there just isn't that much to do anymore now that all the booths are ready. I think Samantha kind of likes to feel important," he said.

That was an understatement!

Billy scratched his head and grinned. "Mom won't care where your booth is," he told me. "Put it on the stage and don't worry about what Samantha says."

That was the high point of my school day, Diary!

The high point of my home day was that Gram stopped by late this afternoon.

So far the Miletti crew has been on its best behavior (except for my argument with Nancy last night). Of course, it's only been one day, so I guess we don't deserve any medals yet, but we're determined to make things easy for Mom.

Josh actually made a list and stuck it on the refrigerator! It's all very neat, a sort of grid with the chores written across the top and our names down the side. Rose has to answer the phone and the door, and bring in the mail. Nancy and I were assigned cooking (among other things), and Adam got the dishes.

"Every night?" Adam complained. "I don't see why I have to do it every night. Why can't we trade off like we usually do? Besides, how can I clean up the kitchen after breakfast? I have to go to school."

"Get up earlier," Josh suggested. He was on his way out with Sebastian.

I waited until he'd left. "Don't worry, Adam," I said. "Just pretend to go along with the list. It'll make him feel good. We'll trade off like always, we just won't tell him."

"Oh. Right." Adam slugged me on the arm. "Good idea, Lizzie."

So except for Darcy, who got assigned dusting, and feeding the animals, we all pretty much agreed to ignore the list. As long as everything gets done, who cares?

So far in my life, I haven't discovered the joys of cooking. I know about the joy of eating, but cooking isn't one of my favorite things. Besides, I never think much about food until my stomach growls. I decided to make Josh happy by trying to be organized, so I sat down at the kitchen table with a pad and pencil and tried to think up a few days' worth of dinner menus.

I'd come up with soup and salad, soup and sandwiches, and sandwiches and salad when there was a knock on the back door.

"I'll get it!" Rose hollered, racing into the kitchen. "It's my job!"

Gram came in with two big pans and a kiss for Rose.

"Gram!" I said, hopping up. "Am I glad to see you!"

"Well, what a nice greeting, Lizzie." She set the pans down on the table and held out her arms. Let me give you a hug."

The hug felt so good, Diary, I almost started crying right on the spot. Gram doesn't miss much and she didn't miss the shaky breath I took to keep the tears back.

"What's the matter, Lizzie?"

"Oh, just . . ."

"Lizzie doesn't like the list," Rose announced. "And she has to cook."

I had to laugh at that. Gram looked at my face for a minute and then she smiled. "Well, you don't have to cook tonight," she said, pointing to the pans she'd brought. "There's a baked ham in that one and dark cherry brownies in the other one for dessert."

"Much better than soup and salad," I said.

"Oh, I don't know," Gram said. "Anyway, you can have ham sandwiches tomorrow night." She held me by the shoulders and looked at me again. "Can I help, Lizzie?"

"Maybe." I knew she didn't mean help with dinner. Gram and I don't have any trouble at all communicating. "Probably," I said.

"Well. Any time."

But that wasn't the right time. Rose was still there and I could hear Mom coming in from the living room. Pretty soon the kitchen was full of people, as usual.

We asked Gram to stay with us for dinner, but she had a house to show in an hour. "But be sure to call me if you change your mind about my staying with you, Lynn."

"Thank you, Mother, but I think my crew is going to do just fine," Mom said.

"I'm sure they are." Gram was inspecting the refrigerator door. "Is this the list you don't like, Lizzie?"

"Josh made it," Darcy said. Josh was out paying the paper boy. "I think it's a good idea."

Gram studied it carefully, and started to smile. "Josh must be in seventh heaven with this."

Mom laughed. "He is. But he's just trying to help. Everyone is."

"Nancy, too," Darcy said. "She reads to me every night."

"Yes," Mom agreed. "Where is she, Lizzie, by the way?"

Just as I was telling them, Nancy came back.

Gram gave her a hug, too. "I was just hearing what a big help you are around here."

Nancy blushed. She always blushes when somebody compliments her. "Well, maybe," she said. "I guess."

"And how's the puppet show?" Gram asked.

Adam said it was not bad. Rose and Mom said it was great. Darcy said it was silly, but funny.

"Ralph and I were planning to come to the fair just to see it," Gram said, "but I'm afraid we both have to show some houses that day."

"That's okay, Gram," I told her.

"Well, I know," she said, glancing at her watch. "I have a little time now. Why don't you give me a private showing? I really would love to see it."

Nancy and I looked at each other and sort of nodded. I don't think either one of us felt like it, but we didn't want to disappoint Gram. We couldn't do the whole thing, of course, so we just did one scene — the one where the new teacher starts crying. It was the first time we'd actually used the puppets and it took a while to get used to them. The socks were much easier.

But Gram laughed at the scene and said once we got the puppets working a little better, it was going to be wonderful.

"Who knows?" she said. "Maybe this will be the start of a puppet partnership between you two."

That'll be the day, I thought. "Well, maybe," I said.

"And maybe not," Nancy said.

I wanted to glare at her, but I knew she'd probably do something childish like stick out her tongue at me, so I just turned away.

I knew Gram noticed that. Like I said, she doesn't miss much. But all she said was, "Thank you, girls. And good luck at the fair." Then on her way out, she casually added, "Lizzie, I know you're extra busy now, so if you need anything, be sure to call."

I guess I'll have to talk to her soon, Diary. It always helps when I do, and I'm sure not working things out by myself!

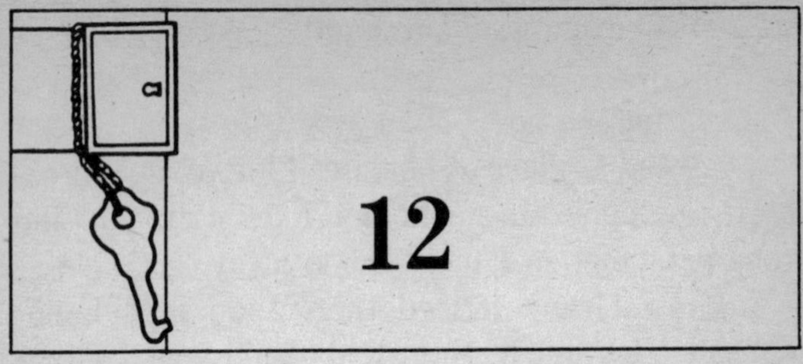

Dear Diary:

After Gram left yesterday, I had a gigantic panic attack about the puppet show. It was Thursday already, and we'd only actually rehearsed the entire thing one time. And that was with socks!

I'd been studying our script, and I was pretty sure Nancy had, too. But we hadn't gotten together and practiced. Ha. We hadn't gotten together and done anything since about three days after she came to stay.

After dinner, I motioned Nancy into the family room. "Look," I said. I was too worried to try being diplomatic. "We were lucky with Gram — that's the scene we know best. But we have to practice the whole thing as many times as we can. We've only got tonight and tomorrow left."

"Okay."

Did you ever hear such an *un*enthusiastic response?

"Come on, Nancy!" I cried. "Even if you're mad,

think about the fair. You don't want us to make fools of ourselves, do you?"

Nancy went over and picked up two puppets. "I said okay, didn't I? You're right, we need to practice, so let's do it."

For a second, I thought about making an extremely dramatic gesture — like ripping the stage and the puppets into pieces and just forgetting the whole thing. Who cared whether there were nineteen instead of twenty booths?

But I guess big dramatic gestures aren't me. Or maybe I'm just afraid of looking silly.

So we practiced, and the first time was a disaster. The puppets kept falling off our hands, and Darcy, who was watching, kept saying she could see our heads.

"Get down, Lizzie," she said. "I can see your hair sticking up. It looks like a big fuzzy spider."

I gritted my teeth and scrunched down. So did Nancy, who's taller than I am and had much farther to scrunch.

"How's that?" I called out to Darcy.

"Good, except your puppet's tilted."

I straightened my wrist and we went on. My arms were getting tired and I felt like my knees were drilling holes in the floor. We kept missing lines and getting our arms tangled and bumping into each other, but finally we finished.

"Well?" I popped up and looked at Darcy. "How was it?"

"You didn't use your funny voices very much," she said.

"What do you mean?"

"You just sounded like Lizzie and Nancy most of the time."

"She's right," Nancy said. "We were too busy trying to remember everything else."

Darcy slid off the chair and walked toward the door. "Nancy, can we read now?"

"No!" I yelled. "Darcy, go read to Rose or ask Mom to read to you. We have to get this right!"

"Don't yell at me!" she yelled.

I took a deep breath. "Okay, Darcy, I'm sorry. Would you watch it again and tell us how it goes?"

Darcy had her stubborn look on. She probably would have said no if it was just me asking her. But Nancy said, "We can read later, Darcy, after I do my homework. Okay?"

Darcy rolled her eyes and sighed, but she said okay. Mom came in then, so we had two in the audience the second time.

"How was it?" I asked when we were done.

"Very good. It was a little rough in places," Mom said, "but I'm sure you'll work that out. There's just one other thing I noticed."

"What?"

"Well, you just didn't seem to have much energy," she said. "You sounded kind of . . . flat. Are you girls getting enough sleep?"

"Oh, sure," I said quickly.

"Tons of it," Nancy added.

At least we were together on that, Diary. Mom has enough problems without knowing that our friendship might be coming to an end.

Adam biked to school today. So did Nancy. They even raced for a couple of blocks, and I could hear them laughing as I trailed along a block behind. I was wearing my winter-white skirt and oversized light blue sweater. The skirt was my excuse for not riding when Adam asked me why I didn't.

This day will go down as one of my worst, schoolwise. By the time I got there, my skirt was spattered with mud. I don't know how it happened. Maybe I was splashed by a car. Anyway, I didn't know it was there, and I probably would have gone through the day happily ignorant about it if it hadn't been for Polly Hart.

"Ooh, Lizzie!" she called after me as I walked toward homeroom. "Your skirt looks like you sat in a mud puddle or something."

"Ooh, Lizzie!" Donald Harrington squealed. "Ooh, Lizzie!"

Donald was making fun of Polly, but he managed to get the entire hallway's attention. Naturally, I felt like everybody's eyes were aimed at the back of my skirt.

I'm never cool in situations like that, Diary. I know some people would just laugh it off, but I always wish I could drop through the floor.

The next bad thing was history. This isn't news, of course. But did Mr. Burrows have to assign a special project? Why do all teachers like special projects so much? Isn't it enough that we have our regular work to do?

"Now that we've finished the chapters on Westward Expansion," he said, "I'd like to see some good projects on any aspect of it that appeals to you."

As you know, Diary, *no* aspect of history appeals to me.

Tanya Malone stuck her hand in the air. "Is this going to take the place of a test?"

The rest of the class cheered, but I knew it was just wishful thinking. Nothing takes the place of a test.

"No," Mr. Burrows said, "but this will count heavily toward your grade. This isn't an extra-credit project."

I could see Nancy thinking about it and I knew she'd come up with something really great. Usually she helps me think of one, too, but I knew I'd be on my own on this one.

Lunch next. Nancy sat by herself. She told Ericka she had to do some extra reading for English, and maybe it was true, but I knew she was using it as an excuse not to sit with me. Actually, she wasn't by herself. Tanya Malone was sitting at the same table, but they were at opposite ends and they didn't talk. Nancy didn't read much, either. Mostly she stared out the window.

"Look at Nancy," Candace remarked snidely. She and Samantha and Jessica were next to my table. "She's so in love, she's spending every waking moment dreaming about Mister Wonderful."

Jessica giggled, but Samantha frowned at them and they both clammed up.

"What are they talking about?" Ericka asked me.

"They're just jerks," I said.

"That's not news," Ericka laughed. "But Nancy being in love is. What's that all about?"

"She's not in love," I told her. "She's just acting like a jerk, too. I don't want to talk about it," I said.

"Okay." Ericka ate some more. "I can tell the roommate situation isn't rosy. How's the puppet show?"

"Don't ask."

"Well, I hope it's better by tomorrow," Ericka said. She finished her sandwich and grinned at me. "I plan to get a front-row seat."

* * *

I hope the show's better by tomorrow, too, Diary. After school today, we practiced again. Two times. I think it went okay, but I couldn't tell.

Mom didn't watch this time. For once, *she* was reading with Darcy. It's a good thing she didn't watch, either, because except for our lines, Nancy and I didn't say a word to each other and Mom would have noticed, for sure.

Then it was time to make dinner. I don't even have the words to describe how that went. Now that I think of it, I don't need words. It was a completely silent operation. And it's so awful, being in the same house with somebody you're mad at and not having any place to escape to.

So later I took steps. It seemed like a good idea at the time, but now I'm afraid I've made things worse. If that's possible.

It was getting late and I'd just come in from brushing my teeth. Nancy was already lying down. And this is Friday night, Diary! Late-movie night. Popcorn and talk night! Suddenly the thought of arguing over the stupid light was too much.

"I have an idea," I said. "Since I like the lamp on at night so I can read, I think I'll just fall asleep up in Gram's old apartment. I've been . . ." I started to say I'd been writing in my diary up there, but I caught myself. "I've been thinking of doing that all day," I finished.

Nancy didn't look at me. "Okay," she said softly.

"Well," I said. "Okay."

So here I am, Diary, upstairs as usual. Except this time it's for good. For good until Nancy goes, anyway. At least we won't fight.

It's kind of lonely.

I wonder if Nancy feels the same way.

13

Dear **D**iary:

Saturday morning. Sunny. That means my hair will look okay. It also means lots of people at the fair. I know I won't be seen, but I'm wearing my soft green blouse with the scalloped collar that makes my eyes look even greener. Jeans, of course, because I'll be on my knees. I'm glad my hair is cooperating. I hope Nancy and I do.

Saturday evening. The fair's over. Is my eleven-year friendship with Nancy over, too?

First, the fair.

Carrying the stage to school wasn't as simple as it sounded. By the time Nancy and I finished lugging the thing there, we were hot and sweaty. I could *hear* my hair starting to frizz. So naturally, the first person I saw was Billy.

"Here, I'll give you a hand," Billy said.

"Thanks," I puffed. "It's not heavy, it's just *big!*"

Dear Student,

We are very pleased to have you back in the SonLight Club once again! Thank you for re-enrolling and please let us know if you have any questions about your Bible lesson. Try to do your lesson the week that you receive it and return it as soon as you can. Because of your re-enrollment we have given you 500 bonus points and your pencil will be sent September 1, 2007. We are very glad to have you back!!!

The SonLight Club Team

The three of us sort of sidestepped down the hall and into the cafeteria, where everyone else was setting up their booths. We set our stage down just inside the doors and looked around.

The first person I noticed was Samantha. She was wearing tight white pants and an oversized top with gold metallic threads in it that made it shimmer. Her hair was shiny and curly and she had a green ribbon in it. Green and gold, the school colors. I didn't think ribbons were Samantha's style, but that's her trick, I guess. She can wear something everybody else thinks is babyish, and suddenly it's cool again.

Samantha was in the thick of it, of course, ordering everybody around. At least, she was trying to. But most people were listening to a woman who looked about the same age as Mom, with light brown hair. I could tell she was Billy's mother.

"Ready?" Billy said. "Let's get it set up."

The three of us lifted it up and started lugging it toward the stage. That got Samantha's attention.

"Wait!" she called. "I forgot to check with Mrs. Watts about whether it's all right for you to be up there or not."

I heard Nancy make a gagging sound, but Samantha ignored it.

"It's probably too late now," she said. "I mean,

everything's all organized and I just don't know . . ."

"It's okay," Billy told her. "I checked with Mom about it. She said it's fine."

"Oh." I could tell Samantha wasn't too happy that we were getting our way, but she recovered quickly and gave him a big smile. "Thanks, Billy," she cooed.

We got the stage onto the stage and Billy said, "Okay. I've got to go help Mom out, but I'll come back and see the show. Good luck."

Well, there we were, Diary. Behind the curtain with nobody to talk to but each other. I took the sign I'd made and set it up in front of the curtain. THE KLAREMONT KRAZIES — A PUPPET SHOW, it read. FEATURING WELL-KNOWN AND MUCH-BELOVED PERSONALITIES FROM CLAREMONT ELEMENTARY SCHOOL. A DIFFERENT SHOW EVERY HALF HOUR. DON'T MISS A SINGLE ONE!

That's all there was to do, really. Except wait. Maybe we shouldn't have bothered to get there so early.

"I guess I'll walk around a little," Nancy said, after we'd made sure there was enough light, and that all the puppets were still in one piece.

I wanted to remind her that the fair started at ten-thirty. But I managed to control myself, Diary.

By ten o'clock, when Nancy wasn't back, I started to worry. I told myself not to, but I couldn't help it. I just wanted this thing to go smoothly and be over.

By ten-fifteen, the noise level in the cafeteria had gone up a few decibels. I opened the curtain to see if I could spot Nancy. I couldn't, but I did see fifteen little kids standing just below the stage, clutching tickets in their hands.

"Can we come see it now?" one of the little boys asked.

"It's not time yet," I told him. I was glad we had an audience already, but I couldn't start without Nancy. "In fifteen minutes," I said, crossing my fingers that she'd show up in time. "Watch the clock."

Nancy came back at exactly ten-twenty-five. By that time I was a nervous wreck.

"Where were you?" I asked.

"I was just walking around outside," she said. "We've got five minutes, don't we?"

"But there are people waiting already!"

"Lizzie, I'm here! Okay?"

I took a deep breath. Be calm, I told myself. We can't fight now, of all times.

Four minutes later, twenty kids filed behind the curtain. Out of sight behind our stage, we waited for the shuffling to stop.

I stuck my Principal puppet up. In my stuffiest, deepest voice, I said, "Welcome to Claremont Elementary School."

Up popped Nancy's Kid Bully puppet. "Ha!" she shrieked. "You think this is just any old school? Well, it's not. It's the Klaremont Kraaazzzyy School!"

That got a laugh, and the show was on.

The first show went great. I guess the worst thing would have been to hear dead silence, or else a lot of yawning and shuffling around. But mostly we heard giggles, and at the end, the kids clapped real loud.

I hadn't forgotten about Samantha's booth, of course. Before we did the second show, I took a peek into the cafeteria. It was really crowded with parents and hundreds of little kids running around to every booth.

But it wasn't just little kids. There were a lot of older kids, too. And just as I expected, most of them were buying bracelets and hanging out with the beautiful Samantha.

Okay, so a puppet show wasn't as cool as friendship bracelets. Maybe we could make a lot of money, at least.

The second show went fine, too. It was during the third one that trouble started.

"Waahh, waahh!" I sobbed, bobbing my Teacher puppet up and down in my left hand. The little kids seemed to like this part a lot.

"Don't cry," I said, changing voices and patting my left hand with my Nice Kid puppet. "Klaremont's not that krazy."

"That's what you think," said Nancy in her Kid Bully voice. "Do you know what happens to new teachers here?"

Instead of waiting for me to say "Wh . . . wha . . . what?" in a scared voice, she went on, "They wind up in the same room with — Kid Detention!" and she popped up a mean-looking puppet clutching a (mini) baseball bat.

My Teacher puppet was quivering with fear, and I was supposed to say, "Wh . . . who . . . who's Kid Detention?"

Nancy didn't wait for me to get my lines out. She just kept barreling along with hers.

The audience was laughing, so I whispered to Nancy, "What about my lines?"

"Sorry, I got carried away," she whispered back. "Never mind, just keep going."

I guess I was rattled, Diary, because I forgot my next line.

I finally remembered what I was supposed to say, and we went on. But in the next show, Nancy got ahead of me again. Plus we crashed into each other and her knee wound up mashing my leg.

"Ow!" I whispered. "You're killing me!"

"Well, move over!"

"How can I when your knee's pinning my leg to the floor?"

Somehow, we both managed to fall down while we were getting untangled. Then our stage started to shake madly, so we both had to grab it, and our puppets disappeared for a few seconds. The audience seemed to think this was part of the show, but I wasn't laughing along with them.

"We don't have much room back here, you know," I said when the show was over.

"I know, I know," Nancy sighed. "Could you just relax, Lizzie? This isn't Broadway, you know."

"Relax? How can I relax when you keep making me forget my lines?" I said.

"I didn't mean to do that," she said. "But if you weren't so jittery, you'd be able to improvise."

"Improvise?" I hissed. "I'm not any good at that. That's why we wrote a script!" I started rubbing my leg. "I think I've got a bruise."

"Oh, will you stop moaning?" Nancy said disgustedly.

I was still rubbing my leg when I noticed that Billy was peering at us over the top of the stage. He looked a little worried, and I didn't blame him.

"Hi," he said. "Sorry. I didn't mean to listen, I just . . ."

"Don't worry," I told him.

He pushed his hair back and smiled a little. "Can I do anything? To help with the show, I mean?"

"Sure," Nancy said. "You can tell Lizzie to stop being such a worrywart."

"Worrywart?" I said. "When did you start using an expression like worrywart?"

"Just now," Nancy snapped.

"Anyway," Billy said, interrupting us. "I just came to tell you that everybody's coming to the next show. Most of the kids in our class, I mean. I thought you might want to know."

While Billy was talking, I could hear our next audience coming onto the stage. Even without looking, I could tell they weren't first- and second-graders. Their shoes were a lot heavier, for one thing, and they didn't giggle and whisper. They hollered corny jokes and insults at each other and then howled at how funny they were. It was my class, all right.

I bobbed up and looked. Ericka, Tanya, Polly, Donald, Robert, they were all there. Then I saw Samantha and Candace. I guess they left Jessica minding the booth. Samantha had that superior smile on her face, and I just knew she was expecting us to fall on our faces.

My stomach started doing backflips, and I felt so scared, Diary! Maybe I shouldn't care so much what other people think of me, but I do. I wanted to tell Nancy, so she could say something like,

"Don't worry. We'll be great." But, of course, I couldn't.

Well, I don't know how we did it, but we got through the show without a single mistake. And we were great, both of us.

After it was over, everybody came back to talk and compliment us.

"That was really fun!" Ericka said.

"Very nice, very nice," Polly said, as if she were a newspaper critic.

"Yeah," Donald agreed.

The fair was almost over by this time, and Billy had to go help his mother again. But he gave me a big smile and said it was great.

Even Samantha made a comment. "That was so sweet, Lizzie," she said.

I knew that was more like a pat on the head than a compliment. She was trying to feel superior again. But I didn't care. We'd been a hit with our worst critics.

If this had been a movie, Nancy and I would have turned to each other and smiled. We'd be feeling happy, happy enough to make up, wouldn't we, Diary?

Well, it's not a movie, and even though we were both feeling happy (I was, anyway), there was no big make-up scene.

Instead, we had another fight. Not at the fair.

We went through the rest of our shows and even got home before it happened.

I'll call it the Spaghetti Snarl.

After we got home and told everybody how the show went, it was time to make dinner. I checked my list of menus (it *does* make things a little easier), and saw spaghetti and salad. Nice and simple.

I put the sauce on to heat and the water on to boil. Nancy started a salad. I went upstairs to change my clothes. When I came back down, the water was boiling, so I threw in the spaghetti. I could see Nancy outside, talking to Adam and Darcy and Josh. Mom was out on the front porch with Rose, waiting to catch the first glimpse of Dad's car as it drove down our street.

The phone rang, so I went into the family room to get it. It was a wrong number. As soon as I hung up, it rang again. Same wrong number.

You can guess what happened next, Diary. By the time I got back to the kitchen, the spaghetti water was bubbling merrily, up over the top of the pot and down the sides, into the flame. I could hear the hissing even before I hung up.

Nancy and Adam came indoors then. A lot of the water had boiled away, and the noodles were a gooey mess.

"Didn't you hear the phone ring?" I said as I started cleaning up.

"Nope."

"Sure, because you were outside," I told her. "I had to answer it and I couldn't watch the spaghetti at the same time."

Nancy was mopping up some of the water that had spilled onto the floor. "I guess you should have turned it off," she said.

"Me?" I cried. "What about you?"

"Hey, you guys," Adam said.

"You shut up, Adam Miletti," I told him. "This is none of your business."

"Holy cow," he said disgustedly. "What's your problem?"

"It's me," Nancy said.

"Huh?" Adam looked totally confused.

"Never mind," Nancy said. Then she looked at me. "Don't worry, Lizzie Miletti. I won't be your problem much longer."

After that, she ran up to my room. I told Adam to slice some of Gram's ham for dinner, and I came up here, Diary. I guess I'll have to go down when Dad comes home, but I'm not looking forward to it.

I have the feeling this is going to be a very cold dinner, in more ways than one.

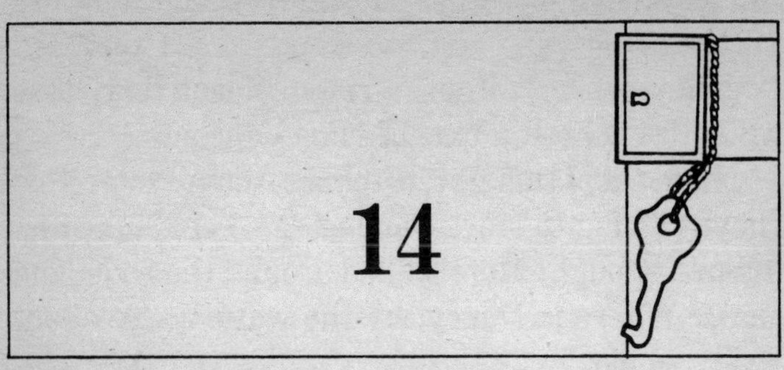

14

Dear Diary:

It seems like a long time since I wrote last, but it was only yesterday. So much happened, and I don't know what to tell first.

After the Spaghetti Snarl, when I was in the middle of the longest, sniffliest cry I think I've ever had, Dad came home. I heard him honk when he turned into the driveway — three toots, that's his signal — and I knew I had to go downstairs. I also knew I looked like a complete mess. I could tell my eyes were puffed up like balloons and I knew my nose was like Rudolph's. I just hoped everybody would have the good manners not to mention it.

The first thing Darcy (who else?) said when I got into the family room was, "What happened to your face? It's all splotchy."

"Allergy," I said, thinking fast.

"Well!" Dad rubbed his hands together. He's always happy to get home. "First, thanks, kids, for helping your mother out. She tells me you were all terrific."

"They were," Mom agreed. "I couldn't have asked for a better bunch. Nancy included."

Oh, great, I thought, catching Adam's eye. Now they're going to start wondering where Nancy is.

Sure enough, Mom looked around the room and said, "Where is Nancy, by the way? We're about ready to eat."

"Um . . . well," I mumbled. I can't seem to think fast two times in a row.

"She went out," Darcy said.

"On her bike," Rose added.

I gave Adam a questioning look and he nodded at me. She must have gone to the nature preserve, I thought. Or to her house, to get the mail again. Or just for a ride, to get away from me.

"Well," I said cheerfully, "she probably wanted some fresh air, after being stuck behind that puppet stage all day."

"Oh, yes, the puppet show," Dad said. "Tell me how it went, Lizzie."

So I told him while we ate. Dinner turned out to be kind of slapped together — ham and salad and pickles and stuff — and we didn't sit at the table, except for Mom and Rose. The rest of us just stood around nibbling and talking.

It's a good thing it wasn't a sit-down meal, otherwise Mom would have started fretting about where Nancy was. You see, she didn't come back. But with everybody moving around like that, Mom didn't make a big deal over it. "I guess you're right, Lizzie. Nancy must be out bird-watching," was what she said. "Let's be sure to save some food for her. She'll be hungry when she gets back."

While I was eating, I made a decision: I'd go see Gram that very evening. I didn't know why I'd waited so long, but now that I'd decided to do it, I couldn't wait to get out of the house.

Ralph and Gram had just finished dinner themselves when I got there. It must have been Ralph's night to clean up, because when he answered the door, he had a big dish towel wrapped around his little potbelly.

"Lizzie," he said, holding the door open, "come in, come in."

"I would have called first," I said, "but I forgot." The truth was, I hadn't even thought of it. I'd just dashed out without even thinking they might not be home.

"Well, I'm glad we're here," he said. Then he looked at my face and I could tell he knew something was the matter. But all he said was, "Why don't you go on into your room, Lizzie? I'll tell Betty you're here and she'll come right up."

"Thanks," I said. Then I reached up and kissed him on the cheek. "Thanks for not asking."

"My" room, the guest room, is decorated in yellow and white, and it's really comfortable and cheerful. Nothing could have cheered me at that moment, however. I sank down on the bed and the minute Gram walked in, I started to cry.

She let me. She didn't say anything or do anything except hand me a box of Kleenex. Finally I sniffled to a stop.

"It's all over," I said.

"The crying?" she asked with a smile.

I smiled, too, a little. "My friendship," I said. "Mine and Nancy's."

The nice thing about Gram is she didn't say, "Oh, of course it's not," or "you're exaggerating," or "it'll work out, you'll see."

What she said was, "Tell me."

So I told her. Everything. All about how I had to keep reminding Nancy of the puppet show. How she wouldn't even give up reading to Darcy. I told her about the dumb night-light and how I'd moved up to the attic apartment. Finally, I told her about Adam.

"And she had the nerve to say I was jealous!" I said. "Not of Adam, naturally. But of her, because she was having fun. I never heard anything so dumb!"

Gram was quiet for a few minutes. Then she said, "Well, I don't know whether Nancy has a crush on Adam or not. But if she does, it probably would have been very hard for her to tell anybody, even you, Lizzie."

"But why?" I asked. "I'm her best friend. At least I was."

"If it's true," she said, "Nancy was probably more surprised than anybody. After all this time of thinking boys are jerks, here she actually finds herself liking one. Maybe she wanted to just keep it to herself for a while, until she got used to it."

"Yeah, I guess I can understand that," I admitted.

"But it might not be true," Gram reminded me.

"Well, I wouldn't care if it was," I said grumpily. "Except she couldn't have picked a worse time, with the puppet show and all."

"Mmm," Gram said. "How did it go today?"

"Great," I told her. "We were a big hit."

"That's wonderful," she said. "Did Nancy really not do her share?"

"No, she did it," I said. "I guess I didn't have to worry so much. It's just that she was always with Darcy or Adam or doing homework and stuff. She never seemed to have time for me. I mean, what's the point of having a roommate if she just becomes one of the family?"

That's when it hit me, Diary. I *had* been jealous. Not of Adam or Darcy or anything like that. I had this nice picture in my head of what a roommate was: somebody who'd only pay attention to me. So when Nancy moved in and didn't act like I expected, I got mad. And I used the puppet show as an excuse.

I looked at Gram. "Having a roommate's a lot different than having somebody sleep over once in a while, isn't it?"

Gram laughed. "That couldn't be truer, kiddo." Then she hugged me. "Why don't you go home now and talk to Nancy?"

Well, Diary, that was easier said than done. Because when I got home, Nancy still hadn't come back. It was almost dark by this time, and Mom was really flustered. When I walked in, she was telling Dad he should go out looking for her.

"She could have had an accident," Mom said. "Maybe she broke *her* ankle, and she's lying out there in that nature preserve with nobody to help."

I never realized Mom had such a vivid imagination.

"I don't think she went there," Adam said.

"Why?" I asked.

"Well, because when she left, she didn't have her binoculars," he said. "She had Oscar. In a box."

"Why didn't you say so before?" I asked Adam.

He shrugged. He's my favorite, Diary, but he can really be thick sometimes.

"Oscar?" Mom said. "She took her cat out riding with her?"

"She didn't go riding, Mom," I said. "I'm pretty sure she went home, to her home. I'll go get her, okay?"

Mom looked like she might argue, so I said, "We had a fight. I have to talk to her. I'll call you when I get there."

Mom couldn't argue with that, so I got on my bike and took off again. I hoped Nancy would at least let me into her house. I didn't like the idea of shouting my apology through the closed front door so all the neighbors could hear.

Because that's what I had to do — apologize. I wonder if I'll ever be good at being a friend.

It was almost completely dark by this time, so it's a good thing Nancy was wearing that old white E.T. sweatshirt or I might have crashed right into her and never had the chance to tell her I was sorry.

She was walking down the sidewalk toward me, carrying Oscar's cat-box in one hand. I swerved to the side and screeched to a stop. I could hear Oscar scrabbling around in the box.

"Hi," I said.

"Hi." Nancy put the box down and shoved her hands in the pockets of her jeans.

"I'm sorry," I said immediately. There was no point in beating around the bush. "I really messed up. I know I'm always messing up, but I always realize it, right?"

Nancy didn't say anything, but at least she was listening. So I told her everything I'd thought about at Gram's. "I just wanted you all to myself," I said. "You know what it's like for me, being in the middle over there. It's like I get lost sometimes. I know I don't, really, but that's how I feel. Anyway, you were right. We could have had fun with the puppet show — with everything — and I was the one who ruined it."

By now I was crying. For the third time that day, Diary! Fortunately, I had a Kleenex with me.

When I blew my nose, Nancy made the gross honking sound she always makes at that moment. That's when I knew everything was going to be okay.

We both laughed a little, and Nancy said, "You really acted like a creep, Lizzie Miletti."

"I know, I know," I admitted. "But could you tell me you forgive me so we can go home? I don't like standing around out here in the dark."

"Why do you think I was coming back?" she said.

"To forgive me?"

"No, because of the dark." She picked up Oscar's box. "I was scared to stay at home alone, even with every light on. I left my bike there — it was too hard to carry Oscar on it."

I started pushing my bike, and we headed back. "So?" I said. "Do you forgive me?"

"Yes, I forgive you, Lizzie Miletti," she said solemnly. "On one condition. You never, ever, ask me to do a puppet show again."

"That's easy," I said. "I don't know if I'll ever even *want* to do one again." Then I couldn't help saying, "I thought you'd make me promise not to tell a soul that you like Adam."

Instead of denying it furiously, Nancy ducked her head and kicked at the sidewalk with the toe of her sneaker. I knew it, I thought. She does like him.

"We're really just friends, that's all," she said. "But I guess I did kind of like him. Not the way Samantha likes boys," she added quickly. "But maybe a tiny bit the way you like Billy."

"What do you mean, you *did* like him?" I asked.

"It just didn't last long," she said. "Maybe because I'm still not ready for that."

I kept quiet. This was the first time we'd ever had a "boy" conversation where she didn't think the entire thing was pukey.

"Don't tell Samantha," Nancy said.

"I hardly even talk to Samantha," I reminded her. "Anyway, don't tell her what — that you liked Adam or you don't anymore?"

"You can be so dense," she said. "Don't tell her *anything*. Just let her go on thinking Adam and I like each other. It's been kind of fun, having the Snob Queen jealous of me!"

We both cracked up at that, Diary. And much to Mom's relief, we were still laughing when we walked into the Miletti Fun House.

15

Dear Diary:

It's Tuesday night. Nancy's mother got back yesterday so Nancy has gone home.

Saturday night when Nancy and I walked in, Mom was so relieved to see us both laughing that she let us break out a bag of potato chips. We don't get much junk food at our house, unless you count the stuff from Roth's. Which I do!

I could tell Mom wanted to ask me a thousand questions, but she didn't, and I was grateful. I didn't want to go into every awful detail about what a rotten friend I'd been.

All she said was, "Are you okay, Lizzie?"

"Everything's fine, now," I told her. "I just goofed again, as usual."

She laughed and shook her head. "You don't goof half as much as you think you do."

"She goofed today," Darcy announced. "At the puppet show. She and Nancy fell down."

"I didn't think anybody could tell!" Nancy cried.

"I could," Darcy told her. "Because I saw you

do it right, here at home. But it was okay," she added. "It was real funny. Not just the falling part. The whole thing."

After that, we sat around talking about the show, and Dad told about his trip. Rose fell asleep in the big stuffed chair and Dad carried her up to bed. Then he helped Mom upstairs.

Up in my room, Nancy and I got into our pajamas. Actually, I wear a big blue-and-white striped nightshirt, and Nancy wears a Smurfs T-shirt.

"Look," Nancy said, holding out the potato chip bag. "There's still a lot left. Want me to go down and get something to drink?"

"I already have something." I showed her two of Darcy's juice boxes I'd brought up. "You'll just have to resist the urge to pop them," I said. Nancy loves to stamp on empty juice boxes and make them pop like firecrackers. It's one of those kid things I've decided she might outgrow by the time she's eighteen.

"What good's a juice box if you can't pop it?" she said. "You're no fun."

"I am too fun, Nancy Underpeace!" I said. And just to prove it, I tossed my pillow, and then *her* pillow at her.

We had a great pillow fight, and then we polished off the potato chips and talked. We didn't go to sleep until two-thirty in the morning.

It's too bad I took so long to realize why I was mad, isn't it? I wasted most of the two weeks.

Monday at school, everybody was still talking about the fair.

"I'm happy to announce," Ms. Basley said in homeroom, "that we took in over two thousand dollars."

Whistles and foot-stamping from Donald. And Nancy. Loud cheers from the rest of us.

"Yes, Samantha?" Ms. Basley said.

"I'd just like to thank everyone who helped make it a success," Samantha said.

"Since when were you in charge?" Donald asked her. "Billy's mother ran the whole thing. Let's hear it for Mrs. Watts!"

More cheers. Billy caught my eye and smiled, Diary. Nancy saw it and crossed her eyes at me. At least she didn't make her gagging sound. Maybe she won't anymore, now that she's liked a boy a "tiny" bit.

Samantha had to clap, too. Everybody knew she hadn't been in charge. "Well, I helped her," she said. "And I want to thank everybody who bought my bracelets. We sold them all, isn't that great?"

I did notice a lot of them on people's wrists, Diary. Little kids and older ones. I suppose I should be glad, since the money went for a good cause. But it's hard to be noble when you can't stand somebody.

I guess I don't need to tell you that Nancy and I didn't buy one of the bracelets. But a funny thing happened when we were walking to school this morning. Adam was with us again, by the way, and Samantha noticed. Nancy and I looked at each other and started giggling. That disgusted Adam, who probably won't walk with us again for a long time.

Anyway, after Adam went on toward his school, something in the gutter caught my eye. I was pretty sure I knew what it was, but I had to bend down to make sure.

"Playing in the mud again, Lizzie?" Donald shouted as he walked by.

"Ha, ha." I said. Not a brilliant comeback, I know. But I was more interested in what I'd seen.

"What *are* you doing, anyway?" Nancy asked impatiently.

"Getting this," I said, and I held up one of Samantha's friendship bracelets. You could hardly see the colors anymore because it was covered with dirt and some wet leaves were sticking to it.

"Huh," Nancy said, looking at it. "Samantha would be insulted if she knew one of her 'fabulous' bracelets wound up in the gutter."

"Mmm," I said, brushing it off.

"Well, come on," Nancy said. "You can throw it away inside. The bell's about to ring."

But I didn't throw it away, Diary. I kept it. And when I got home, I buried it at the bottom of the junk drawer in my desk.

I didn't tell Nancy. And of course, I would never tell Samantha. I kept it to remind me of the two weeks when I finally had a roommate and almost lost a friend.

Good night, Diary.

Will Lizzie's lie get her out *of trouble, or* into *more? Read* Dear Diary #6: The Lie.